The Ash Beneath My Feet

Lucia Fudge © 2014

For Barrie and Clare

December 1968: Bringing Down Snow

"I'm not going to marry, Mama. I'll stay with you forever."
"You are too young to say such things." Claudia caressed Alexandra's cheek with her sticky hand. "My seven year old baby."
"But I've made up my mind. I'm going to work in a library and live with you."
"My Professoressa of books."
Twilight illuminated the garden.
Alexandra sat on an upturned bucket and stared at her mother. Somehow, she made her bucket seat look stylish. Her long, brown-gold hair was twisted into a bun, drawn low at the nape of her neck. A pendant attached to a gold necklace lay in the hollow of her neck. It caught the setting rays of the sun and illuminated her skin.
Alexandra stretched out on the grass at her mother's feet. It was scorched brown, with threads of green shoots. She plucked out a new blade and felt its smooth surface.

Claudia was silent as she worked. They were surrounded by brown glass bottles, stacked in rows. Claudia lifted one and sprayed water into its neck with the garden hose. Alexandra gave her a handful of small stones and Claudia dropped them inside. She shook the bottle vigorously and Alexandra listened to the swish of the stones against the glass. Claudia emptied it and wiped the surface on a tea towel. At her feet lay a large bowl, filled with diced tomatoes. She lifted the wedges of chopped tomato and slid them down the neck of the bottle. It filled rapidly in her hands.
"Alexandra, it's time to work. You lie like a sheep in the grass, too much time you spend thinking. In my village, we call the men who think and don't work ' pappamolles'."
"But you never finish working. That's why I'm never gunna get married."
Claudia handed Alexandra a bottle.

Cicadas screeched in the dusk air. Alexandra imagined them hidden on tree trunks and bushes, as they called out their summer scratch-scratch song.

She stared at the grass beneath her and pictured the cicada embryos underneath the soil, listening to their ancestors' song above.

"They only live for two days, Mama."

"What do, Darly?"

"Cicadas. They live underground for seven years, then they live above the soil for two days. Then they die."

"Two days is too long! I didn't know where I was when I arrived in this country, even the insects seemed to complain about it."

Alexandra leaned her head against her mother's knees.

"In my country, we have birds that sing in the summer, not crying insects."

"Do you miss Italy?"

"Always, my heart is there." She stroked Alexandra's hair. "You were born in the land of grey trees and kangaroos. In my country, the trees are full of green leaves and they fall down in the cold air. But here, only lightning make leaves fall down."

Alexandra stared at her mother's hands. They were calloused, the knuckles swollen and twisted. Claudia's fingernails were stained red with tomato peels and threads of chopped basil were caught inside her nails. Most fascinating of all, her hands shook with a mild tremor. Alexandra watched as they rested on Claudia's lap.

"Tell me a story."

"You and your stories, Alexandra! We must keep working, otherwise we waste our day. The heat will make us lazy."

"Please."

Claudia stroked her hair again. "You have an old heart, made for listening." Alexandra watched her hands again as she spoke. "I once knew a boy who was made of gold." She held her hand over her eyes to shield them from the glare. "It's cold now in my village, the snow is very deep on the ground. All the way to the mountains."

"I can't imagine snow at Christmas! You couldn't go to the beach or have fun outside."

"Alexandra, you don't know what you talk about. I loved to walk in the forest with my sisters, it was so white, we felt we were walking in a cloud. We would sing, to see if we could make snow fall from branches with our voices. There was a mountain behind our village, Mount Maggiore. We would climb as high as we could, to see if deer were hiding in the forest. My mama said it was good luck to have a deer run before you. She said its innocence would protect you from the evil eye."

"Did you ever see one?"

"No."

"What about the boy made of gold, did he see one?"

"She's thinking of the secret" Alexandra thought. "I can tell by the way she smiles. One day, when I'm big enough, she'll tell me." She watched as Claudia filled the bottle to the brim with tomato slices.

"Well?"

"He did once." Claudia wedged the rim of the bottle with chopped basil and then sealed it with a cork. "He told me that one night, he came back from collecting firewood and a noise behind him made him stop. He look but didn't see anything. Then behind him, a dark shape ran into the trees and he saw it was a deer."

"Was it good luck to see one behind you?"

"You ask so many questions! Not like Pina, she hates stories of our old country."

"Did it bring him good luck?"

"Can I tell my story? You make me forget what I have to say."

Alexandra was silent.

"My sister, Oliva, she could sing like a cuckoo. She would walk to a tree that had small branches, so it wouldn't be so hard to have the snow fall down. But she couldn't do it, her voice was too soft."

"Did you make snow fall down, Mama?"

"No, I didn't have a big voice either. Our cousin would come with us and he could sing like an angel. He always brought down snow with his strong voice. He could do anything. Roland would tease us, said we were paper girls, too soft. He would stand under a giant tree and begin to, how you say? Hmm, like that."

"Hum."

"Si. And the snow would fall and he laugh when it fall on us. Oliva, she gets angry and start to throw snow at him and we hide behind trees and throw at each other." Claudia's eyes crinkled as she spoke.

"Was Roland the boy made of gold?"

"Yes."

"Does he still sing?"

Claudia wiped her hands on her apron. "Alexandra, tell Papa to put the bottles in the cantina. They're ready." She lifted the last empty bottle and looked away as she collected the stones.

Alexandra stood. "The secret's sad for her today" she thought. She walked around the side of the house and braced herself to enter the garage. It was positioned underneath their modern brick house. The shape of the Holden car and an assortment of tools, were visible in the semi-darkness. She felt the cool concrete beneath her feet as she called out. "Papa, the tomatoes are ready." She moved to the side wall and opened the cantina door. The cantina was built underneath the foundations of the house. It ran the length of the house and had a dank, earthen smell. She shivered as the temperature dropped.

"Hey, Pop."

Emilio looked up from his bench. "Mama's finished the bottles, eh? I'll come soon." He turned back and his lean shape blended into the earth. Alexandra stared as he lifted a cane basket onto a high shelf. The rough-hewn shelves were nailed into the foundations of the house. The basket was overflowing with garlic and potatoes. Bottles with preserved tomatoes, peaches and apricots were stacked on the lower shelves.

A floorboard creaked above them and Alexandra started. She looked about the dark space, waited to see a long shadow in the recesses. She imagined a druid lived somewhere in the cantina. It watched her father as he brought it offerings of his summer harvest. One day, if she were quick enough, she would catch its eye. An earthen, insatiable eye, greedy for more offerings. She shivered and her father laughed.

"You read too much, Alexandra. Too many monsters live in your imagination."

She scampered away, back to the golden rays of her mama's love.

Chapter 1: 2010

She was suspended in the wait for Kate. Again. Her most critical decisions were made in waiting bays, she mused. Airport lounges and check out queues. Alexandra stood under the arrivals board and searched for the flight number. Gate ten.

Sydney Airport was serene in the early morning light. New skies softened jet plane emissions, a more forgiving dawn shielded 21st century turbulence. On the horizon, planes ascended and descended like futuristic metal birds, glittering in the early sun.

She passed a flock of thin fashionistas, their frames wrapped in signature black.

"Thank God I'm too old for stilettos" she thought. She stared at the expensive leather that encased their slender feet and glanced down at her own sandals as she walked to the gate. Her sandals held her broad toes in sensible unison, a brace against their tendency to curl under if barefoot.

"Well, how am I?" She wondered, knowing her friend would ask. "Am I amused, resigned, upbeat, content, sombre or reflective? What degree of truth do I present?"

Tourists trickled out of the arrivals gate. A pair of disheveled tourists appeared.

"Young British backpackers." Alexandra assessed the tall couple passing her, striding towards the luggage carousel, their hands held together. "Promise there." She looked away to the next couple. "Grandparents visiting, I sense a reunion."

Alexandra watched a young woman with a pram walk towards the older couple. The toddler in the pram clutched a bunch of flowers, threatening to upend them in excitement. The young woman smiled as the couple approached, the expression lighting up her tired face. A businessman strode past, hand luggage held assuredly, a zip up suit bag attached to the designer case. He looked ahead, avoiding the seeking eyes of the waiting.

"Alexandra."

She turned in the direction of the familiar voice.

"Still watching people, I see."

"Hey you," Alexandra bent to hug Kate, aware that she quickly scanned her shape before looking into her eyes. "You look just the same. I can't believe it's been ten years."

Kate gripped her hand luggage and motioned for the teenage girl behind her to follow. "I look like shit and you know it. Isabella, take the camera bag. Did you say hi to Alexandra?"

A shy nod in return.

"Good to see you, Bella. You've grown so tall, like your dad. How was the flight?"

"Horrible, the man beside me snored all the way from Hong Kong."

"Kate, she has your bone structure. She looks like Wedgewood China too."

Kate lifted her hand case. "C'mon, let's see if our luggage is unloaded. Thanks for picking us up. Mother offered but I knew Isabella wouldn't make it to her 16th birthday if that old hag drove us home. I can't believe the R.T.A. gave her a license for another year. She either bribed the examiner or she slept with him."

"Mum, that's a horrible thing to say! Gran's really old and you make her sound like a tart. Bet you wouldn't say that to her face."

Alexandra replied. "She would. I've heard her say worse in my time."

"No wonder she hates you."

Kate muttered. "She deserves it. I can't believe we're going to live with her for the next six weeks. It's been twenty-five years since I've slept more than a week under that roof. Not enough distance even with those numbers."

Alexandra stopped as they walked ahead of her towards the carousel. "Six weeks?" she called out. "You didn't say that in your email."

Kate turned and quickly walked back to her. "Yes," she spoke in a low voice. "I need a base to get sorted out. Nicholas and I separated six months ago."

"What! You didn't let me know any of this."

"What's to say, I'm going through a difficult time and my life's crap? I've absorbed the English spirit over the last twenty five years; never complain and never explain." She checked to see if Isabella was nearby. "I'll fill you in later. I don't say a huge amount in front of her because we don't know if it's permanent. Nick moved out so we've had the flat in Kensington to ourselves. It hasn't been too bad for Bella because of that." She shook her head. "Well as bad as it can get when two people can't stand being near each other for more than an hour at a stretch."

Alexandra stared at Kate's hazel eyes. Her expression was difficult to discern.

"OK, we can leave it for now."

Kate linked arms with her. "It's so good to see you. How are you? No overseas holidays in the last decade, huh? Are you so important to the bank, they couldn't spare you for a few weeks?" "Things came up, you know what it's like. Anyway, on my salary I can only afford to visit London if I stay with you. Perhaps you'll let me stay in the flat while you're here?"

"No chance," Kate glanced backwards again. "Nick's moved in while we're away. If we sell it, we'll get a better price if we do some repairs. The heating system has to be replaced and the bathroom looks like a teenager's ran amuck with a can of mould." She smiled and the expression relaxed the tension on her features. "Mother's bathroom will be spotless, of course, a 1950's monument to housewifely economy. I wonder if the toilet doll is still there? No, I know it will be, I wonder in vain."

Kate turned to Alexandra. "My God, listen to me! I haven't even seen her and I'm raving already. You'll have to rescue me, lots of nights out to escape the place."

"You make me feel twenty years old again. You always rescued me back then."

"I did, didn't I? Someone had to, and if it wasn't going to be a knight on a white stallion, it might as well have been Katie. Does your mum still call me that?"

Alexandra nodded. "There's a lot of unfortunate things about my mother's memory and that's one of them."

"Tragic, that." Kate hesitated. "I don't know if I'll last that long at Mother's."

"You've put up with worse. And anyway, it's a great opportunity for Bella to get to know her gran."

"Stop being so positive, it's very annoying." Kate stepped back and looked at Alexandra. "You look good, I can say that truthfully. I'm distraught and haggard but you look young and fresh. And I know how old you are. How are you?"

"You asked me that already."

"Did I? What was your answer?"

"Content. Middle aged and content."

"Good for you, Alexandra." Kate called over her shoulder as she walked ahead. "Received any letters lately?"

Alexandra froze, as people jostled for space around her. The baggage carousel clicked into life and the mechanical motion played in her ears. She processed the question, then filed it into a recess of her mind. It rested there, forbidden.

Chapter 2

"Should we drop in and see Kit Kat?" Alexandra turned into New Canterbury Road as she spoke.

"Is she still at Dulwich Hill?"

"She and Bill have renovated the house. It looks fabulous."

"How many years has she been there now?"

"About twenty, I think. They bought the house after I got my flat." Kate fixed her eyes outside the car window. "If you like, you know her better."

"Rubbish, we all went to Uni together. You still have that thing with her?"

"I just never clicked with her like you did."

Isabella called out from the back seat. "Mum, we should go straight to Grandma's. You haven't called her since we landed."

"Relax, child of worry. Grandma won't know if we stop off for an hour somewhere."

"I'll tell her."

Kate turned to Alexandra. "See what happens when you let your ovaries demand offspring? Said offspring turn on you. It's the eternal dilemma of a teenagers' mum: should I reason with my child or just strangle her?"

Alexandra stopped at the lights. "I'd prefer the first option. I've just had the car detailed."

"Of course. Offspring of mine, obey your mother. If you don't, I'll kill you when you get out of the car."

"What are you on about?"

"Nothing, as usual. Just sit and be quiet."

Isabella stared out the window. "Look, everyone's got a huge garden! None of my friends have this at home."

"No one could afford to in London, apart from the Queen. You pay ten pounds per blade of grass. A courtyard's a luxury in London."

"We don't have one."

"We can't afford the luxury." Kate leaned forward, whistling softly. "I don't believe it, this area looks the same as when I was a teenager. I feel sixteen again."

"You don't look it, Mum."

Alexandra turned into a cul-de-sac and pulled up in front of a federation house.

Kate clutched her arm. "Are you sure she won't mind us dropping in unannounced?"

"No, I said we might." She turned to Isabella. "Just half an hour, I promise."

The girl climbed out of the car and bent her head in the fierce light.

Kate watched her. "Your sunglasses are buried somewhere in the suitcase, I'll dig them out when we arrive at Grandma's. I forgot about the sunlight here." She stared at the row of 1920's bluestone cottages. English suspicion of the colonial landscape was evident in the architecture. Each house had small lead light windows, positioned cautiously away from the sun. Verandahs shuttered out northern light, and native trees were uprooted in favour of English cottage gardens. Climbing roses hung wilted on trellises in the midday sun.

"The more things change...." murmured Kate.

Alexandra pushed open the picket fence gate. "Careful! Don't quote that bloody philosopher to Katrina, it used to drive her insane."

"It didn't take much, I remember. Don't worry, I'll behave."

Ahead of them, the front door jerked open and a tall, long-haired woman ran down the front steps. She bounded to a halt and whistled. "This can't be Isabella! Wow, aren't you an English beauty. Kate, she's so like you."

Katrina clipped her hair behind her ears. Her brown and grey hair lapped at her shoulders and forehead and threatened to obliterate her face with its abundance. "Come in. It's been so long."

"Thanks. We won't stay long. I can't believe it's the first time I've been here. All my previous visits were too brief to see you."

"When were you were last in Sydney?"

"Not since Isabella was a toddler."

"Well, you look wonderful. The English lifestyle agrees with you. I've aged heaps since I had the kids, I never get around to colouring my hair. It's a shocker." Katrina pulled at her roots.

"Tom likes you natural." Alexandra replied.

"He's lucky I'm low maintenance, I save him a fortune. He wouldn't notice if I did anything, anyway." Katrina led them to the back of the house, to a cathedral ceiling living area.

Kate wandered around the room. "This is gorgeous, Katrina."

"You like it?"

"Absolutely, I wouldn't know what to do with all this space in my flat. Well done."

"Thanks. We added the back area for the kids. Now they're close to finishing their studies and leaving home. I don't know where the years went."

"I know what you mean. What are they studying?"

"Sarah's in second year nursing and Pete's doing H.S.C."

"Will he go on?"

"I don't know, he's got Tom's rebellious bones. I think he'll pick up a trade, I can't see him at uni."

Alexandra laughed. "He was always a feisty little kid. Remember him at Sue's wedding? He climbed the outdoor trellis and nearly brought it crashing down. The poor Celebrant looked ready to collapse."

"She was OK. Tom plastered her with champagne at the reception."

Kate stood back at the shared reminiscence. She stared at the walls and Katrina caught her glance.

"Do you like the prints? Tom picked them up on a business trip to Hong Kong, they were so cheap. I love the Impressionists."

"They pale compared to the originals. I take Bella to the National Gallery regularly and we just stare in awe at the works. We also visit galleries on weekend trips to Europe."

Isabella interrupted as she helped herself to biscuits laid out on a tray. "It's sooo boring."

"She hasn't inherited my love of art" Kate laughed. "I want to feel the paintings with my fingertips. Never do it though. I'd have my face in the Times for all the wrong reasons."

"That would have been all the more reason for you to do it twenty years ago!"

"Aren't we all changed though."

The quiet reply caused a lull in the conversation and Alexandra turned to Isabella. "What do you want to see in Sydney?"

"I'm not sure."

Kate nudged her. "Go on, tell them."

"What?"

"You want to meet a life guard at Bondi Beach. Preferably male."

"Not just. I want to climb the Harbour Bridge and go sailing and see a ballet at the Opera House. My ballet teacher said it's good to check out provincial culture."

They laughed and Kate shook her head.

"Her teacher's a bloody snob but Bella loves her. Nicholas says I dislike her because she's an Aussie basher. Probably true."

"How is he?"

Isabella glanced at her mum as she replied. "Same as ever, too busy to notice he's too busy."

"He's not visiting this time?"

"No. Is Tom still in sales?

"Sales Manager now. He's always in meetings when I call to meet for lunch. I seem to have become a work widow, just like you."

"Are you teaching?"

"A couple of days a week. It's good grocery money. I like having a few days at home to myself during the week."

"You were always a home bird." Alexandra squeezed her arm. "And you did a great job with this place."

Katrina looked at Kate. "Still live in the flat in Kensington?"
"I couldn't imagine living in the suburbs." Kate stopped. "We sacrifice space for convenience. There's always a trade." She smiled. "Have you and Tom travelled much?"
"Just a bit within Australia. Now the kids are older, we'll have more opportunity. I just have to convince Tom to take some time off." She looked away as she spoke. "You were always keen to be off on an adventure."
"My adventure meter pegged years ago."
Katrina was silent and Kate stood and edged closer to the hallway. "We should go. Mother will be pacing up and down and calling Qantas by now."
Katrina stood. "Thanks for dropping by. You must feel shattered after the flight. We'll catch up soon, you and Isabella must come over for dinner. I've learnt all sorts of decadent Greek recipes from Tom's mum. That woman's ruined my hips for life."
"I'd love some home cooked Greek food. It's not the same in London, doesn't compare to the Greek Isles."
Katrina didn't reply. They walked down the hallway and Alexandra pulled Kate over to the wall. "Remember this?"
Kate leaned closer. "You kept it, Katrina! I can't believe it, I haven't sketched in over twenty five years."

Katrina stayed silent as the two women stared at a print on the wall. It was bound in an unvarnished wooden frame. A pencil sketch of a bush picnic, the background a soft line of ghost gums and wattle. In the foreground sat a young woman, her hair and clothes a collection of exuberant, gypsy layers.
Alexandra snorted. "What were we thinking? Those eighties fashions were hideous. Look at your hair, you look like Sheena Easton!"
"I know. And the shoulder pads, did we need them under tee shirts as well?"
Katrina spoke quietly behind them. "I put it there because it matched the colour of the wall. I haven't looked at it in years."

"Of course. It's nice to see it again. Come, Bella. We must go."
Isabella remained motionless as she stared at the print. "Did you do that, Mum?"
Alexandra smiled. "She did. We thought she was Norman Lindsay that day." She squeezed Kate's hand. "You really should have kept it up."
"Too many visits to the National Gallery cured me of artistic pretensions. I could sketch but if I couldn't be brilliant, then I didn't want to be a middle of the road, bourgeois artist. There's enough out there already. Come, Bella."
White glare greeted them at the front door and Isabella bent her head again as they walked to the car.
"The light's so different here, it's like a lovers slap across the face." Kate spoke. "It beckons you in England. You need to quicken your pace to capture it, it hides and retreats behind clouds and shadows." She shrugged her shoulders. "What homeland am I homesick for now?"
Alexandra nudged her. "We'll send you back when we get sick of your musings over bad weather and crappy food."

Ahead of them, Katrina opened the front gate.
Kate stopped at a rose bush and she bent to absorb its scent. "Such fragile perfection," she murmured. "How transient and trivial is mortal life; yesterday a drop of semen, tomorrow a handful of spice or ashes."
Katrina whitened at her words and strode past them to the front door. She opened it and didn't look back as she entered the house.
Isabella looked puzzled. "Did you say something wrong, Mum?"
"With her, I always do. Let's go." She looked at Alexandra. "I did my best. The Marcus Aurelius quote just slipped out."
Alexandra nodded and they walked to the car in silence. Her stomach churned and she felt claustrophobic, for no apparent reason at all.

Chapter 3

"There you are, Darling. I was beginning to worry."
The metallic screen door obscured the view of the person behind it. However, the voice was firm and clear.
"Mother."
"Isabella! How you've grown. Or perhaps I've just shrunk more. Do you know that's a scientific fact? Old people shrink each year as the cartilage in their bones reduces." Rosemary's bright eyes searched them. "You'll be greeting me at knee length in five years time."
Alexandra laughed. "You look marvellous, Rosemary."
"Good thing you compliment me, my daughter never does. Do you?" The octogenarian eyes shone from behind the screen. "What a minute, I'll just find my keys."
Alexandra stared at the frayed cane chairs near the stairs as they waited on the porch. "Are they the same cushions as twenty years ago?" She whispered.
"Yes," Kate whispered back. "Welcome to the twilight zone."
"What are you girls whispering about?" A hand appeared on the door, the knuckles gnarled and twisted. Liver spots lined Rosemary's white skin. She stooped towards them. "My mother taught me never to whisper. If I couldn't say something aloud, it wasn't worth saying." She clutched Isabella's arm and the girl bent to hug her.
"Hi, Grandma."

Kate bent towards her and briefly brushed her cheek with her lips.
"Mother, you do look well. Isabella has grown lots; she got Nick's bone structure. Thank Heavens, if she had ours, she wouldn't grow much over five feet. We wouldn't wish that on her."
"Well, I've always managed being short." Rosemary stroked Isabella's pale skin. "You're a pretty girl. Get that from your grandma, you do. Come inside, I have tea ready in the lounge."

"The place looks the same as when I was last here. I think I left that teacup on the sideboard there."

"Perhaps you did, Kate. Remember, I was never much of a housekeeper. The garden held such charm for me, I was never inside long enough to dust and polish. Always seemed a waste of time to raise dust, then let it settle again. Seemed to be more sensible to be out in the garden, with the growing things. Your father loved a tidy house, I always felt I let him down on that score."

Alexandra watched Kate as she sat on the sofa. She resembled a coiled animal, ready to spring. "I've got your gene there, Mother. I never gave a toss about housework. Fortunately neither did Nicholas. We only worried that we'd lose Bella as a toddler under the piles of newspapers and dirty washing. She was a clever monkey though, always managed to wiggle out of the disorder and make her own in the process."

"A clever child indeed. What do you do to fill your time if you don't do housework or gardening?"

"I work. I time share the marketing supervisor's job four days a week."

"I worked full-time after your father died. Still managed to keep the garden immaculate and attend to the minutia of household things."

"Less the cleaning."

"Very well, we've discussed that."

Alexandra shifted closer to the edge of her chair, her body tense. "Twenty five years later, and they're still in the Hall of Mirrors." She thought. She remembered the first time she had sat in this room as a University student and listened to their conversation. She had on her lap a modern history book. The cover showed a collage of political figures at the Palace of Versailles. Tall, bewhiskered men in long waistcoats. Beneath their quill pens, on crisp paper, lay the war reparations meted out to the German nation as punishment for the 1st World War. She felt them haunting this room, as a modern detente continued between Rosemary and Kate.

She started back to the present as she watched them. "They still hammer out negotiations to end their private war. The same reparations demanded, the same shuttlecock repartee." she thought.

"Grandma, I like to garden."

"Do you?"

"Yes, I plant the seeds in our window boxes. It's my job to water them. Dad says if we left it up to Mum, they'd die in a week." Isabella looked at her mum, who cleared her throat.

"I should tell you, Mother. Nicholas and I separated six months ago."

An antique clock on the mantlepiece chimed the half hour, a sweet, old fashioned sound.

"Why on earth didn't you tell me before? Isabella could have used some grandmotherly love, even if you didn't need me."

Tears welled in Isabella's eyes and Kate lifted her eyebrows.

"We'll talk about it later. What's new in the garden; planted any natives yet?"

Rosemary lifted a glass of water to her lips and Alexandra thought she saw a tremor in her hand.

"Why on earth would I do that? I've always had a cottage garden, I don't like those sparse, grey bushes. Reminds me of heath. I always found that drab as a child."

"They use less water, you wouldn't be forever sprinkling the beds. Perhaps Bella could plant some with you, she'd love her own patch of soil. Wouldn't you, Blossom?"

Isabella leaned forward, her eyes shining. "We had garden beds at school last summer, for Home Economics. Each class could choose their own vegetables and herbs. It was brilliant!"

"How lovely," Rosemary smiled. "You can help me choose seeds tomorrow at the nursery. It's a long walk and I'll use your young legs to push my trolley. I think you'll come in handy." They smiled at each other. "We'll leave the natives for now though, throw too much shade on the flowers."

Kate stared out the window. A magnolia tree flowered directly in front, its scent blocked by the sealed window. Dappled sunlight filtered onto the carpet, added depth to the faded pattern. "The light was always so pretty in this room," she murmured. "I played with my dolls on that window sill. I pretended the flowers were presents from the garden fairies, left behind to sprinkle magic on my dolls. You kept the window open in those days."

"Your father was still alive then, so I felt safe. I wouldn't dream of doing that now, with all the break-ins in Strathfield." Rosemary spoke. "You were such a fanciful child. Shame you never pursued that artistic side. Still, I'm glad Isabella has her father's pragmatism. Dreamy children are so hard to manage."

Alexandra motioned to the clock. "I've always loved that time piece, makes me think of the "Hickory Dickory Dock" rhyme. A mouse should scurry upwards on the hour chime."

Rosemary laughed. "With my housekeeping standards, perhaps one does. How are your parents? I never see them now I don't go to the markets."

"The same, just older and fatter. I'll be as fat as Ma one day."

"Nonsense, you were always a sensible and disciplined girl. Though I do remember when you and Kate went on the apple diet at university! I despaired of Kate, she weighed next to nothing and refused all my best casseroles and puddings. I hope you don't do that to your mother, Isabella. A good appetite is a sign of mental health."

"I must have been disturbed then." Kate stood up. "We'll take our cases to the spare room, Mother. You stay with Alexandra, we won't be long."

"Darling, I've given you my room. It's bigger and you each have a bed. I'm happy in the spare room."

"I don't want it." Their eyes locked.

"Now, don't be like that. I've had the carpets steam cleaned and laid out new sheets."

"No."

Rosemary shrugged at Alexandra. "I don't understand why it's always like this."

"Bullshit!"

Isabella jumped at the word.

"You know I don't like sleeping in your room."

"Nonsense, Kate. It's just because he read to you in there."

"Don't second guess me. Isabella and I can stay at a motel."

"But I want to stay with Grandma."

The clock chimed again, bereft of mice and sweet rhymes.

Alexandra spoke. "Listen, my offer holds." She winked at Kate as she continued on. "I know you don't like to put your mum to extra work, so why don't you stay with me and Isabella can stay with her grandma. I'm not far away." She smiled at the young girl. "Everyone loves a holiday away from Mum. It's like Christmas come early."

Isabella spoke softly. "If it's OK with Grandma."

Rosemary stared at her glass of water. "Well, if that's the best we can do. I did want both my girls to be with me. Seems I won't get my wish, again." She looked at Kate. "It's cruel to have you in Australia but only at arm's length."

"It's better like this. Isabella, help me unpack your things, then I'll head off."

She touched Alexandra's arm in silent gratitude. "Do you need to be somewhere soon?"

"No, I have the morning off. I'll go into work later." Alexandra held her breath.

They sat in silence, suspended in the wait for Kate.

1969

The men began to sing and Pina rolled her eyes at Alexandra. "Oh God," she whispered. "They'll go on forever now!" She stood and attempted to tiptoe away from the raucous group gathered around the outdoor trestle table. Above the table hung a long wire frame, heavy with grape vines. The vigorous plant obliterated the fierce heat of the sun.

Claudia caught her by the waist and pulled her back. "Sit with your sister, she needs company. She's still sick with the bronchitis."

"No, I'm not, Mama. That was last month." Alexandra rubbed her eyes and bent over her book again.

Claudia stood behind Alexandra and gently closed her book. "No more, Cara. You need to rest your eyes for now."

"No, I don't."

Claudia lifted the book from her hands and raised it in the air. "My daughter will be a Professoresa of books. They will be her babies one day."

An older, dark haired woman looked at Claudia with amused eyes. "Wait till she's fifteen! My Lilliana loved to read when she was little but now she only likes the boys."

Claudia smoothed the hair from Alexandra's forehead. "Lilliana is her mother's daughter. You liked to look at boys too when you were young, Rosetta."

Rosetta laughed and raised her wine glass. "Ecco! And Alexandra will love only one boy, there will be no-one else."

A silence fell over the table.

Emilio stood abruptly and clapped his hands. A flock of birds, perched on the sun-bleached fence, flew away. "Steal my grapes, they do." He sat down again and the singing recommenced.

"Once bloody Signore Mario starts singing, we're trapped till midnight." Pina muttered.

She rested her head in her hands as a wiry, muscular man stood on his chair. His tenor voice commenced a ballad and everyone clapped at his choice. A gradual humming of the chorus grew to a swell of voices.
Alexandra never felt a desire to leave when the ballads started, unlike Pina. She stared at her parents' friends. They swayed as they sang, lifting their glasses in the air to emphasis the chorus of a song. Empty, dark green wine bottles lay scattered over the tablecloth.

The words were unintelligible to Alexandra; simple stanzas rising to a strong chorus. Her heart swelled at the longing in their voices. Couples held hands or hugged each other as a new song commenced. Women nodded at the lyrics, their brown eyes filled with memories.
She stared at her parents and waited for them to embrace. They sat side by side, never touching as each song's last note lingered in the summer heat.
"Pina," she whispered. "Do you know Mama looks like an Empress?"
"What? Ally, are you mad?"
"No," she hissed back, "I saw it on TV last night. A man was showing old coins from thousands of years ago and one looked just like Mama. Same big nose and forehead. He said she was from a rich family and had lots of slaves to look after her."
"Wish we still had some," muttered Pina. "I'd have them murder Signore Mario for singing this garbage." She grinned. "I'm gunna try crawling under the table. Maybe they won't notice if I slide away like a snake!"
Alexandra's eyes widened as she watched her sister duck under the table and attempt to negotiate tapping feet as the singing grew more vigorous.
Pina gave the thumbs up as she crawled past the end of the table and hid behind the grapes that grew over the side of the wire frame. She waited until Mario stood on the table again and ran towards the house, her hair flowing behind her.

Claudia's eyes shone with a curious light, neither happy nor sad. Mario commenced a love song and she clasped her hands together and nodded at the lyrics.

Alexandra stared at those mysterious, shining eyes. "She's thinking about the boy of gold," she decided. "She only looks like that when she's thinking about him." Alexandra caught her eye and Claudia smiled at her. Her hear beat faster at the look in her mother's eye and she smiled back. "I can read her mind." She thought.

Emilio stood to clap the birds away and he knocked Claudia's shoulder as he lifted his hands in the air. She turned away from him, then stood to clear away the plates of antipasto, her hands shaking.

Chapter 4

Kate sat in the small, high fenced back garden and stared at the yard. Early morning sun scorched the buffalo grass, reduced the tough blades to a pale yellow sheen.

A Spartan collection of plants in terracotta pots lay on the grass, long abandoned to the sun. The Art Deco building threw permanent shadow over patches of the lawn. The deep green colour of the shaded grass set it apart as a protected species, favoured by chance. "It's like a rebuke from a pagan god." Kate gazed at the sunlight as it lit the landscape with piercing clarity. "Harsh and unforgiving."

"I thought you'd sleep in." Alexandra opened the back sliding door. Her still-black hair hung thickly on her shoulders as she moved across to the outdoor table. "What degree of shocking do you feel?"

"What do I look?"

"Absolutely shocking."

"That covers it. I was awake at six this morning, it was so light in my bedroom."

"I know, my flat's on the Sydney obsessed north-eastern corner. I had to fight at auction to buy it."

"Too vivid an image at this time of the morning."

"I'll put the kettle on." Alexandra stepped into the adjoining kitchen and rummaged for mugs.

Kate motioned with her hand. "You've done a stylish job on the flat."

"You like it? It doesn't look post-modern, ironically sophisticated?"

"Like my flat in Kensington, you mean? No, it's a decorative summary of Alexandra Suplina."

"Too obscure for my ears this early in the day."

"I mean every object in this flat describes you. I was with you the day you found that sewing machine."

"I remember! Ten bucks at Vinnies. I don't know how people dump that kind of precious stuff, it's a 1920s Singer."

"I know why. Perhaps it reminds them of their mother."

"You were horrible to her yesterday. Why you both can't drop the antagonism and get along, I'll never know."
"I'll never forgive her."

Alexandra handed her a mug and motioned for her to sit in the lounge room.
"Much more comfy, those cast-iron garden seats are murder on my back. I've got to lose five kilos or I'll start walking like Quasimodo."
"Do you still have your collection of old books?" Kate walked to the bookcase and scanned the shelves.
"As if I'd give them away! Kate, for someone as soulful as you, sometimes you've got no soul."
"I know, I'm the heartless sum of many neurotic parts." She ran her fingers over the leather bound volumes. "I should have known, no Jackie Collins here."
"None in your flat either, just lots of obscure philosophy books."
"Now you're getting personal."
"My claws are soaked in love."
"Bullshit."
 Kate knelt on the floor and examined a low shelf. It was crammed with faded editions of classic English literature. She brushed a hand over the volumes as she spoke. "Are you pleased with your life?"
"What do you mean?"
"You know."

Alexandra shifted on the sofa. She stared at the coffee table and remembered the day she found it at Lifeline. The relish she felt as she took it home and coated its aged patina with beeswax. She focused her eyes on the surface as she replied. "With what I have physically, yes. I could always reshape a piece of furniture. I'll never achieve what I wanted emotionally. Anyway, it's been so long, I don't know that I want it any more. I'm forty nine this year."
"Ancient you are."

"You'll always be more ancient than me. Don't forget you're six months older."

"Of course. What do you wish for?"

"I'd like to pay out my mortgage, see Europe before I need a walking frame."

"Apart from the shopping list, what do you wish for?"

"Kate, I don't think like that anymore.....I'm not twenty years old, I know the deal."

"What is it?"

"You're so annoying." Alexandra stood. "Want another cuppa?"

"Please." Kate turned sideways, away from the sunlight and curled her legs up on the sofa. "I'm just like her," she thought. "I no longer seek the light either."

April 1981: University of NSW

"Do you think it's been here since 1965?" Kate lay on the floor and kicked the scuffed beanbag away with her small feet. Her white-blond hair spilled over her shoulders, half-hid her almond shaped eyes. "Dunno, it's not the kind of antique I'd collect." Alexandra sat on the floor, leaning against the wall, her coffee in one hand and study notes in the other. The student room was deserted. Used cups littered the floor and cigarette butts overflowed in the metallic ashtrays.

Kate stared at her. "What do you wish for?"

"Pardon?"

"Y'know, what do you want out of life?"

"You're not really big on superficial conversation, are you?"

"Are you?"

Alexandra laughed. "A question answered with a question. Are you a Greek philosopher, reincarnated?"

"Are you? You just answered my question with a question."

"You're strange."

"I try to be," Kate gave a small smile. "Above all, do not distract or strain thyself, but be free and look at things as a man, as a human being, as a citizen, as a mortal."

"Ah, what particular philosopher are you channeling now?"

"Marcus Aurelius."

"Lived?"

"AD 121."

"I see."

"You didn't answer my question."

"Which one, Kate? There's so many."

"What do you wish for?"

"Short term, to pass my linguistics exam. Long term, world peace and an end to famine."

"You're being facetious."

"Of course I am. I only met you a month ago, I'm not gonna tell you everything. What do you wish for?"

"Lots of sex with gorgeous men."

"You've got a better chance than me."

"Nonsense, you're tall and very attractive."

"Rubbish, I look like a woman in a Picasso painting, all swarthy and hairy."

Kate laughed and rolled over on the floor in a sultry fashion. Alexandra looked at her. "You, on the other hand, are as dainty as a piece of Wedgwood China. I'm the original bull in the China shop."

Kate looked up, then gasped. "Oh, shit!" She flung the beanbag over her upper body and whispered. "I've got to hide. Cover my legs, now!"

Alexandra draped her long legs over her automatically and pretended to read her notes. She glanced up at the sound of footsteps and saw a boy in the doorway look enquiringly within, then walk away. He had long, curly hair and a sweet, wistful air about him.

"He's gone, you're safe."

Kate lifted her head cautiously from underneath the beanbag. Her hair spilled over her face and the wild tangle added to her petite beauty.

"Why'd you want to hide from him? He's bloody gorgeous!"

"I know but he's a churchie." Kate smiled at Alexandra's curious look. "A born-again Christian. He waylaid me in the Blue Room after my English tutorial. I thought he wanted sex but all he did was talk about what Christ meant to him. I was so disappointed, I couldn't speak for half an hour. Then I told him I was a Stoic with Pagan leanings. He told me Stoicism was a root of early Christian thought. All I could think of was that I'd like to take a root from his Christianity."

"Is that sacrilege? Should I burn you at the stake for that?"

"There you go again, asking as many questions as I do. You're a born philosopher, Alexandra."

"Alex."

"No, Alexandra. It's so pretty and feminine."

"Said by you, yes. By my Italian father, no. It's sounds like a meat dish on a restaurant menu."

Kate laughed. "Anyway, you can't burn me at the stake. It's illegal and I'm vegetarian. The smell of burning flesh would make me puke."

"A Stoic vegetarian with Pagan leanings. That's a big handle for a tiny girl."

"I've always had big ideas. I plan to study my masters in London."

"I never see you study. Unless you're a genius and don't need to study, how to you intend to achieve Honours?"

"Plenty of time to catch up."

"Do you have family in England?"

"Yeah, lots of half-dead rellos. What about Charlie gadding about with that Spencer girl? I think he'll marry her, where else would he find another virgin in the world?"

"He could always marry me."

Kate glanced at her. "Oh, I see. We'll have to amend that situation as quickly as possible."

"Are you gonna set me up with the churchie?"

"God no, you'll wait forever. Lots of lustful young men on campus to fit the bill. How old are you exactly?"

"I'm twenty."

Kate rolled over and threw the beanbag at Alexandra, knocking her study notes out of her hands. "We've got to get you into the 20th century, my girl. It'll be my personal mission this year." Her eyes assessed Alexandra as she murmured. "Love nothing but that which comes to you woven in the pattern of your destiny."

"Marcus Aurelius again?"

"Yup."

"You know, you're getting kinda annoying."

They grinned at each other, then Alexandra picked up her study notes again and scanned them.

Kate lay on the floor, staring out the window at the sunshine.

Chapter 5

Kate sat on the floor of Alexandra's lounge room and looked about her.

"Bet she hasn't been in a retail shop since 1980." She positioned a cushion behind her back as she leaned against the hard frame of a 1930's cane sofa. She examined the walls.

"No heartless reprints here."

An early 20th century Vogue magazine cover hung on the opposite wall. It was of a model wearing a flapper style dress, cut to mid-length. Her dark hair was cut in a bob and her eyes were darkened by kohl. Her carefree smile beckoned a new age for her peers, she was the glamorous suffragette of her generation.

A series of smaller prints hung underneath in witty contrast. Each print encapsulated the 1920's Australian housewife; a slender woman sewed with her electric machine and another baked a cake under electric light. Smiling, freckled children ate factory-processed biscuits and washed in Pears soap. A photo of a soldier from the Great War hung at the end. It seemed to admonish the gaiety of the other prints. "Lest we forget."

An oak dining table with bulbous legs and four, brocade balloon chairs was positioned in a corner of the room. On it, a crystal vase was filled with dried lavender. An antique Chinese cabinet, its brass locks and seals battered by age, stood behind the table.

Directly above her, a mahogany shelf held a collection of photo frames and Kate stood to examine them. Black and white photos of a subdued war bride and groom, solemn children and an old woman stared directly at the lens. Unknown people, all precious to the collector. Crystal rosary beads were placed in front of the photos, their sheen reflected on the glass frames.

"She still prays," Kate whispered, "to silent gods." She turned away and a solitary print above the Chinese cabinet caught her eye. She walked over and peered at the small frame. An exquisite moment of release within her.

"She kept it!"

She examined the print closely. It was a pencil sketch of a young woman. She sat, hunched over on a grassy lawn, knees drawn up and head tilted downwards, as she read a book. Behind her, a blurred tree line and a distant stone sculpture. The girl was oblivious to her surroundings, her profile youthful and serene.

Kate backed away from the print and wiped her eyes, as somewhere within her a foreign emotion welled up.

Chapter 6

The automatic door closed and Jenny muttered underneath her breath. "Bloody customers! The bank would run so well if we didn't have any."

"I heard that," Alexandra brushed past her head teller. "Are you mutinying? I'll make you walk the ATM plank for that. You can balance the machines for a month on half pay with no lunch break."

"Alex, cut the 1970's bank manager talk. All you need is sideburns and a pair of flares. We know you hate customers as much as we do."

"Let's not tell them that. Anyway, you can't grumble on a Friday afternoon. Who's staying back for drinks?"

Six hands shot up behind the counter and Alexandra grinned.

"All of us, it seems. Jen, can you go to the bottle shop and pick up a bottle."

"Or two."

"I'm afraid the petty cash doesn't stretch that far. We'll have to chip in for another bottle."

"Done."

"Why can't you display such keenness behind the counter?"

"Because none of us gives a shit."

"Just pretend you do when the Area Manager arrives next week for our yearly audit. We came tenth last year. My job's on the line."

"You said that last time. Is Frank staying back?"

"I hope so, he usually pays for the extra bottle. Are we selling truckloads of insurance?"

Jenny spoke. "Alex, this is Balmain, home of the free spirit. Do you know how hard it is to sell an insurance policy to someone with dread locks?"

"Yes, I process their personal loan applications. There's two classes in Balmain, the old money crowd and the broke hippies. It's always been that way."

"It's not our fault we only get the hippies."

"That's why they sent me here, Jen. To send me grey before my time."

"We've been meaning to talk to you about your hair."

"Enough, back to your hovels and sell, sell, sell. I want to win manager of the month. I could go in the draw to win a holiday if we sell fifty policies."

Jenny gave a dry laugh. "The Gold Coast is so exotic this time of year. You'll bump into all the Balmain hippies."

"Well, I'll see if I can rope Frank in to pay for the plonk." Alexandra walked around the narrow counter and stopped at the doorway of a corner office. "Knock, knock."

At her voice, a tall, slump-shouldered man looked up from his desk. He looked a comically accurate version of a bank manager. "Something you need, Alexy?"

"Frank, the staff are in desperate need of morale and alcohol. Got any?"

"No, but at least we can buy alcohol. Drinks on later?"

"Yeah, everyone's staying back."

He looked at her. "You look tired. You haven't got a private life happening on the side?"

"Frank, what a question to ask me! You know I live for my job."

"Good, it would be horrible if I was the only person in this branch without one." Frank put his hands behind his head and put his legs up on his desk. "I need a holiday. Come away with me to Paris."

"Are you serious?"

"No, but we could go to the central coast, I've got a holiday flat there."

"You scoundrel, leading me astray."

"Someone's got to."

She sat across from him. "I've got someone staying with me who did in the past."

Frank's eyebrow shot up. "Really, long lost boyfriend?"

"No, a girlfriend I've known since uni, Kate. You've heard me mention her before, the one who lives in London."

"The pretty, artistic one?"

"Yeah. It's amazing how good a man's selective memory can be at times."

"Bring her into the office."

"She wouldn't look at you."

A hurt look crossed his face. It was a sweet, uncomplicated face, still unlined in its fifth decade. A friar's wedge of hair clung near Frank's ears, as if conscious of its receding proprietorship.

"Sorry, Frank. That was mean of me. She's not your type, anyway. Kate was gonna stay with her mum but they have a tortured, oh so English relationship. So I now have a lost soul staying with me for a while."

"Shit, now you live and work with them." Frank leaned back and patted his abdomen. "My nephew asked if I was pregnant. Said I looked like his mummy before she had the baby."

Alexandra tried to look serious.

"Go on, laugh. I can see you're dying to."

"I told you to take up bush walking with me."

"Some bloody sympathy you show me."

"It's pretty funny."

"Wasn't at the time, the whole family were there. Bastards started laughing, then my brother-in-law ticked me off for not losing weight. Said I was signing my own death warrant."

"That's a bit strong."

"He's a wanker, always was."

"Join my bush walking club, it's completely wanker-free."

"Please, what would I have in common with a group of fanatics who think walking twenty kilometres a day is fun? Or who crouch in front of a bush if they spot a rare, wobble crested galah?"

"We don't do that!"

He arched an eyebrow and she nodded. "Well, maybe sometimes. Think about it though."

"Let me have the baby first, I'm told breast-feeding's hell."

She stood. "Can you fund the second bottle?"

"You know I don't earn much more than the tellers."

"Pack away the violin. We all know the outrageous bank fees pay management's superannuation funds."

"I think that happens in Switzerland. This is Sydney, home of the impoverished bank manager. However, I do have a spare ten dollars."

"Marvellous, we can all look forward to a vintage bottle."

"Dismissed. Go and earn my superannuation with the general public."

She headed towards the door.

"Alexy."

"Yeah?" She turned back.

"Don't overdo the hospitality with the English broad. Your parents work you hard enough as it is."

"This sounds like a lecture."

"It is."

"Is this part of my employment contract?"

"Yes, fine print on page twenty. Staff are to be bullied by overweight manager, to give him a sense of importance."

"As long as it's in my contract." She left the office.

Chapter 7

The candle threw soft light on the lounge walls. The ice in Kate's glass crackled as she sipped her wine. The prints on the walls were indistinguishable, the flapper was consigned to shadows. The rosary beads shone luminous in the eerie light.

Kate sat on the rug, her legs drawn up, hands between her knees. The warmth of her skin like a siren call, unanswered.

"All of us are creatures of a day." She murmured.

"Hey, you in?" Alexandra's voice sounded from the hallway as the front door opened.

"In the lounge room. Don't switch on the light! Please."

Alexandra appeared in the doorway and dropped her handbag on the side table. "Let's switch the lamp on instead."

"No please, leave it like this."

"Sure." Alexandra sat on the sofa.

"Why are you grinning?"

"Kate, I wish you'd been there. We stayed back for drinks and Frank got absolutely plastered."

"Frank?"

"My Manager, I've mentioned him before. He's always so professional with my staff but tonight, he's having dinner with his family, someone's birthday. Needed some Dutch courage. God, we laughed, he started telling really bad jokes about a French barmaid and an Englishman. The girls were beside themselves. Who's gonna cringe when they go back to work on Monday?" She leaned back. "This looks pretty, Kate. I should have candles more often. Suits the old place."

"I know."

The candlewick tilted and the light moved on the walls. The flapper's arch smile re-appeared and the rosary beads gleam was extinguished.

Kate stood and walked over to the fridge. "Have a glass?"

"Why not, I'm only seeing the oldies tomorrow."

"On a Saturday! Can't you squeeze them in during the week, so you don't give up your weekend?"

"No, I'm exhausted after work and on Sundays I bush walk. It's fun though, Pina, Ted and the kids come over and we catch up."

"Every Saturday?"

Alexandra remained silent as Kate poured her glass. She kicked her shoes off and stretched out on the sofa. The candlewick tilted further and extinguished itself in the wax.

Alexandra leaned sideways and switched the art deco lamp on. The small lamp was encrusted with numerous coloured glass panels. A warm yellow light lit the aged objects in the room.

"I should have bought a better quality candle." Kate handed Alexandra her drink. "The two dollar shops in Newtown are the same as in London. Candles are a one hour burner."

"Never mind, at least I can see again." Alexandra raised her glass "Cheers."

"Same, big ears."

"You went to Newtown today?"

Kate sat back on the rug, knees drawn up again. "Yes, I took Bella. She didn't get it, said it was even dumpier than Portobello Road."

"She's only thirteen, she probably found it weird. Did Rosemary go along?"

"You must be kidding! She doesn't travel five kilometres outside Strathfield. Listen, I can stay in a serviced apartment for now."

"Rubbish, I'm glad to have you here. Did you notice how gentrified Newtown has become?"

"The top end near Sydney Uni, yes. The further down you go, it's the same as ever." Kate sipped her glass. "I called Nicholas today. I hope you don't mind."

"Of course not. All OK?"

"All OK," Kate echoed. "I told him that Bella loves her grandma, thinks she the grooviest octogenarian on two legs." She took a long drink from her glass. "I don't think we'll get back together."

"Why? You've had so many years together. He adores you."

Kate twirled her glass in her hands as she spoke. "Too many silent anniversaries. First anniversary of the affair, first anniversary of the baby's death, first anniversary of when he stopped finding my Australian accent endearing."

Alexandra leaned forward and touched Kate's shoulder. "I'm sorry, I didn't know Nicholas had an affair. That must've been really hard."

"At first it's like a small tear on your heart. It grows quietly, till suddenly it's a chasm and you don't know how you got so far away from each other." She drained her glass and stood abruptly. "Top you up?"

"No, I've had a few already. How's Rosemary enjoying Bella?"

"Grandmotherly bliss. If I never do anything useful for my mother again, I did give birth to Bella." Kate refilled her glass. "They get each other, in a way my girl doesn't get me. When I arrived today, I found them gardening out the front. Bella was wearing one of Mother's cardigans from the sixties and they were as happy as pigs in manure. Bella was talking about a boy she likes at school and Mother was planting seeds alongside her. I felt like I was interrupting an outdoor pyjama party. I'd arrived too late and couldn't break into the conversational rhythm."

Alexandra squeezed her arm. "Poor you. That's a grandmother's privilege, all the fun of loving them with none of the responsibility. My mum spoils her grandchildren rotten. Pina says she needs a stomach pump and a hyperventilation chamber to detox the kids when they get home from a visit. It's part of the deal."

"No, you don't get it. Mother doesn't indulge her; she directs her, gives her jobs and a time frame and Bella laps it up. If I try that at home, she shuts herself away in her room for hours."

"It might relate to the separation."

Kate pointed to the space above the photo shelf. "Do you like it?"

Alexandra focused her eyes. On the cream wall hung a Greek icon painting. It was of Madonna and Child, painted in the traditional elongated strokes of Orthodox icons.

"Her face," whispered Alexandra. "It speaks."

"Doesn't it?" Kate stood and touched the frame. "See the faintly perceptible shadow of grief cross her eyes while she holds her pink infant. Like a silent acceptance of the cross to come."

"Thank you. It must've cost a fortune."

"No, it didn't. A Greek man displays them in his coffee shop in Ashfield. I thought this was perfect for your wall. A nice counterpoint to the rosary beads below, you like that religious paraphernalia."

"You've got me neatly labelled." Alexandra stood and placed her glass on the coffee table. "I'm going to bed. Will you clear up?"

"I've made soup for dinner."

"I'm not hungry, just tired. Too many weekly targets I guess. Goodnight." She walked silently down the hallway.

Kate sat in front of the coffee table and lifted the candlewick from the wax. She pressed it between her fingers and lit a match towards it.

Weak, wan, it lit. The flame tilted on its axis. Kate switched off the lamp and watched the fragile light weave around the walls.

She lifted her glass to the icon.

"Welcome." she whispered.

Chapter 8: Newtown, 1982

"That looks exquisite on you, very regal."

Alexandra flung the shawl off her shoulders. "Nothing looks exquisite on me. Thanks for the pep talk, though."

The shopkeeper turned back to her counter.

Alexandra sat down amidst a sprawl of boxes and old magazines at the back of the shop.

Kate bent down and whispered. "That was so rude of you!"

"She just wants a sale." Alexandra blew on a dusty cardboard box.

Kate sneezed. "I don't know how you can sit in this shop every week. My allergies would go insane. And she did mean it. That shawl suits you."

"It costs forty dollars and she'd like me to buy it. No bloody way."

"You're a rough wog! I can't take you anywhere." Kate glanced at the shabby interior of the op shop. "So this is your fave place to hang out in Newtown."

"Cool, huh?"

"No comment."

It was a long, narrow 19th century terrace. Faded layers of proprietorship were painted over each other. The current incarnation was a bric-a- brac shop of early 20th century wares. Small, dark cabinets lined the sides of the shop entrance, creating a hazardous pathway. Dramatic fur stoles hung over the front doorway. Sequined 1960's cocktail dresses that smelt of spilt champagne hung from wire frames. Art deco jewellery and marquisette watches lay jumbled in black, velvet-lined cabinets. 1920's advertisements for Pears soap and Arnott's biscuits lined the peeling walls.

"The only way to traverse this shop is hopping on one foot. There's not enough space for two." Kate muttered as she pushed her way to another dress rack. "I'll leave you to your Nirvana."

Alexandra nodded. She searched through a cardboard box, piled high with books.

"The thrill of discovery, you never know what's in a box." Her eyes gleamed. "Last week I found an 1890 edition of 'Little Women'. I'm sure Miss Alcott was glad I rescued Jo from this mess."

Kate nodded. "I'm sure she's thrilled that Jo's 20th century twin has her safe."

"Very funny."

"C'mon, Alexandra! Lets try on cocktail dresses."

"No thanks, I'd look stupid."

"I love your spirit of adventure."

Alexandra tipped another cardboard box upside down. Books tumbled to the floor and the proprietor stared at her with thinly drawn lips.

Kate whispered. "You're a shit-stirrer."

Kate turned back to the clothes rack and caressed the aged fabrics with her hands. She sorted the silk, sequins and velvet into a vivid palette of colour.

"What do you think?" she held up an armful of beaded tops and dresses. "I'm trying them all on."

The proprietor sighed in the background.

Alexandra sat cross-legged as she searched a pile of hardback novels. She stroked a 1900 edition of 'Alice In Wonderland' and opened the cover. A mouldy smell filled her nostrils as she stared at the stained sketches of characters. She put the book to one side, lifted another and held the spine up to the light.

"My God," she murmured, "I can't believe it!"

Kate poked her head out from behind a blue calico curtain. "What's up?"

"Come here," Alexandra whispered.

Kate crouched alongside her, a silver cocktail dress zipped halfway up her back. "That old bag's ready to kick us out."

"She won't, I spend at least ten dollars here a week."

"Last of the big spenders. So why'd you drag me out?"

"Look!"

Kate peered at the book's title. "'Sketches by Boz' What's the big deal?"

"You Philistine! Did you see the date or the author's name? It's Charles Dickens' first book, published in 1839, a collation of his short stories. It's marked three dollars! Don't say a bloody word when I'm at the counter. This could be worth a fortune!"

"You're so cute." Kate stood and twirled in front of her. "What do you think?"

Alexandra looked up, her hands cradling the book. "No, you're the cute one. That looks divine on you."

Kate spun around again. "My Reeboks spoil the effect, I know." She twirled her hair into a chignon and pretended to smoke a cigarette. "What do you think, Faye Dunaway?"

"Absolutely. You have'ta buy it."

"It costs twenty five dollars and I haven't bought all my textbooks yet. And it's June! My mother would kill me if she knew."

"Don't tell her. I'll lend you the money, I got paid today from work. C'mon, I'm buying these books." Alexandra navigated the littered floor. She concealed the spine of the books as she placed them on the counter. "I'll take these and the dress my friend's wearing."

"I see." The proprietor punched the amount into the till with a cigarette-stained finger. "Thirty dollars."

"Thanks, Alexandra." Kate met her at the counter and hugged her.

"You left the dress on?"

"Absolutely, I love it. It's never to early in the day for sequins." Kate twirled in her dress, a beacon amongst the faded decor. "Did you get the book?" Alexandra quickly lifted the books into her bag and nodded.

"Imagine," Kate spoke as they walked past the counter, "buying a mint first edition print of the most famous writer of the 19th century, for three dollars! It's probably worth $2,000.00". She smiled at the proprietor. "Have a nice day".

Alexandra ran out of the shop and halfway up the block before she stopped.

"You bitch!" She was laughing. "How could you? I'll pay four times as much now, she'll check every book from now on."

"Rubbish, that old hag hasn't read a book of great literature in her life. She wouldn't recognize one, she'll only mark up the Mills and Boone crap."

Alexandra held the book close to her chest and felt the hard, leathery cover.

"Let me shout you coffee, it's the least I can do for the gorgeous dress. And the most I can afford." Kate turned into a narrow passageway between two buildings and motioned with her hand for Alexandra to follow. Pigeons flew above them, searching for their alcoves. Their cooing echoed in the air, as feathers fell to the ground.

Flowering vines covered a brick wall at the end of the passage. Scented white flowers hung in clumps in the gloomy light. Kate turned to her left and bent under a low wood beam, to enter a small café built at the back of the shop front.

"I never knew this was here."

"The churchie took me here last week."

"Really, have you been reformed?"

"No, but I figured I had as much right to corrupt him as he had to evangelize me."

"Who won?"

Kate didn't reply and Alexandra laughed.

"Good to know you don't score all the horseflesh."

She sat at a table as Kate ordered. Posters of sixties pop icons hung from low walls. Janis Joplin stared out from a ripped poster, her sultry eyes acclimatized to smoky dens. Bob Dylan bowed down low above the front counter. A poster of John Lennon, in bearded, melancholic brilliance.

The shabby chaos charmed Alexandra.

"It's fab, isn't it?" Kate placed a coffee before her. "I always felt as a teenager that I was born at the wrong end of the music revolution. All that disco crap of the seventies was a distortion of something magical that went before, I just didn't know what. Here, you get a glimpse of it."

"You have a lyrical way of speaking."

Kate nodded. "My mum said I'm like a comet crashing in space. I'll leave a brilliant trail and nothing else."

"Nice of her."

"She's a piece all right. I hate her."

"Your dad's dead, isn't he? You never mention him."

Kate bent her head and nodded. Her fringe fell over her eyes as she spoke. "He was divine, so unlike her."

"Everyone fights with their ma. Mine hates me wearing jeans, she thinks I should wear skirts to uni. Can you imagine? She's such a dag."

"But you love her."

"I'm sure your ma loves you."

"No. She didn't love my dad either. I think she had an affair with my uncle."

"That's gross."

Kate watched as Alexandra opened her book and turned the pages with careful hands.

"Have a look at the lithographs! They're by George Cruikshank, Dickens' artist. A rambunctious record of a past world."

"Who's being lyrical now? I can see you working one day in the vaults of the State Library. You'll wear a cardigan and pearls and talk about obscure books with other collectors and live in a state of literary bliss."

"Hope so." Alexandra closed the book.

"We're going clubbing soon. I've got to get you laid."

"I don't think I'll introduce you to my ma. You're corrupting me."

"Hope so."

They grinned at each other. The voice of John Denver sounded in the background, as he sang of love and betrayal in a postmodern world.

Chapter 9

"I don't trust her."

Alexandra turned to her sister. "I know, Pina. You never did."

They sat on the back patio and gazed out at their parents' garden. A quarter of an acre wide, it lay in the basin of Sydney's southwest. A transplanted European garden, of roses, dahlias, orchids and neat vegetable beds.

"Don't worry about Kate," Alexandra continued. "She does her own thing. I barely see her."

"How long's she staying?"

"Six weeks. She and Nicholas have split."

"I pity her there."

A tall, solid man wandered across from the vegetable garden. "Pina, your mum cooks too heavy a lunch. I feel shocking."

"Ted, no one forced you to have two plates of pasta or two serves of dessert. I saw you! There's such a thing as discipline."

"You know I love my tucker."

Alexandra spoke. "We've all noticed that in the last twenty years. Just don't serve the kids the portions we used to get as kids. Remember, Pin?"

"I'm pretty strict about that. This is the only place Ted gets indulged. Ma should watch Dad more, he's starting to look like a barrel on two varicose legs."

Ted jumped up. "You can be so gross! No wonder the kids horrify my parents with the things that come out of their mouths. They're listening to you."

"Go away, I want to talk to my sister. You should've married the Aussie chick who fancied you at uni. She would've given your offspring the social niceties your parents long for."

"No, I wanted to play my part in assimilating the ethnic population of Sydney. Noble man that I am."

He walked out to the garden again and called out to the stooped man pulling weeds from the herb garden nearby. "She's picking on me again. I'll come and annoy you, Emilio."

The older man looked up and shook his head at Pina.

"Now you're in for it," Alexandra murmured to Pina. "Ma would've heard that from the kitchen."

"She's never gotten over her gratitude that he married me in the first place."

"Well, you were a fallen woman."

Pina looked down at the table and traced her finger alongside a wide crack in the weathered wood.

"How's work, still flooded with targets?"

"As always, make maximum profit with minimum staff."

Pina nodded and continued to trace the patina of the table.

"Did Kate have any news about him?"

"No."

"Did you ask?"

"Look, it was over ten years ago and we've both moved on."

"Ok, I won't ask any more. It'd be nice though, to know what happened to him." Pina looked sideways at her. "Hopefully, he was hit by a bus or killed in a plane crash. Y'know, just deserts."

"You're a loyal big sister. Always ready to avenge my heart."

"Well, it's not easy to talk about him with you."

Alexandra looked away. "Look, there it is! The wattlebird's on the fence. Remember I told you I saw one the other day?"

"So it is." Pina replied quietly.

The back door swung open and they both looked up.

"My daughters, now I can rest."

"Sit down, Ma. You've been on your feet since we got here."

"I sit all week with Emilio, like two old birds in an empty nest." Claudia leaned on Pina as she sat down.

Pina stood. "I'll make coffee. Would you like one, Ma?"

"Please, Darly. Make it the Italian way."

"Ted can't drink it too strong, he's got too Aussie a stomach for that. You shouldn't encourage him to eat so much. All he does is complain after."

"In my house, I do what I like. You can feed him rabbit food in your house but not here."

"Pina, I think you've argued this for the last ten years. C'mon, Pavlov. Learn your lesson."

"I'll put salt in your coffee, to match your tongue."

"You should talk."

Claudia called out as Pina opened the back door. "You shouldn't speak to your husband the way you do. One day, he run away with an Australiana and it will be your fault. I never speak to Emilio like this."

Pina looked at Alexandra. "I think the dementia's kicking in early. How some people forget." She closed the door behind her.

"Great lunch, Ma. It's the only pasta I eat all week."

Claudia looked at Alexandra. "Makes me sad when you say that, Alexa. You should cook it all the time." She sighed. "It's all passing away."

Alexandra stared at her mother's profile. It was a mirror image of her own, accelerated in linear years. A Roman nose and thin lips, with a high forehead. Thick, coarse hair swept into a bun at the nape of her neck, with dyed brown tendrils loose around her face. Fine, gold jewellery at her ears and neck. Her olive skin burned by a harsh sun.

"Zio Roberto is very sick. We say goodbye on the phone this week."

"Why don't you go over to Italy? You and Pop can still travel. It'd be fun to see the family again."

"Pah! It's not my home anymore. Last time, we were like strangers. Everyone talks so fast, walks so fast. No fresh air in the city and the village is all gone. What for I go back? To watch the dying join the dead?" She shook her head. "I can do that here. Do you know Rosetta died last week? Week before, she play bingo, then she's gone. No Darly, I stay here."

"You can always go next year."

"I could be dead next year." Claudia pressed Alexandra's hand to her lips. "Gold of mine."

Pina pushed the screen door open with her foot, balancing a tray in her hands. "Ma still talking about death? No wonder you and I have a bleak view of life."

"What, Darly?"

"Nothing. Here's your coffee, super hero strong."

"Good girl." Claudia smelt the aroma. "Perfect."

Alexandra looked at her sister. "See, you're still the perfect daughter."

"Unlike you, black sheep. No husband or children to validate your life. What'll we do with her?" Pina looked at her mother.

"No man good enough for my Alexa."

"Oh please! The way you speak about her..."

"She's making fun of me, Ma."

Claudia watched them. "You're both making jokes of me. I never did that with my sisters, we respect our parents." She clutched her lower back. "My back, it hurts all the time with arthritis." She drained her coffee and got slowly to her feet. "I'll pack some food for you, Pina. You give it to the children tonight. I wish they come to visit more, just like the old days." She headed to the back door.

"She's been saying that for thirty years." Pina looked at Alexandra. "Don't take any shit from Kate."

"You sound like Frank."

"How is he?"

"Same as ever."

"You should invite him for lunch one day."

"You should mind your own business one day."

They grinned at each other in the late afternoon sunshine.

Chapter 10: Taylor Square, Christmas Eve, 1982

"I feel like a tart."

Kate pulled her arm. "It's a bit of lipstick and eyeliner. C'mon, Kit Kat, stand behind Alexandra, in case she tries to run away." Her silver high heels gleamed in the dusk as she walked ahead of them. "Follow me, innocents. I discovered this place with Bill last week."

"Who's Bill?" Katrina whispered to Alexandra.

"Her new boyfriend. Divinely handsome but not very sharp."

"I heard that." Kate turned around. "How can you say that? He's a final year economics student."

"I rest my case."

"He's got a gorgeous nature."

"I heard you mention Stoicism to him last week. He asked if they were a London band."

"A natural mistake."

"If you're a total dweeb."

Katrina spoke. "He must have something else going for him if he's slow on the uptake."

Kate replied. "Look beneath the surface: never let a thing's intrinsic quality or worth escape you."

"Stop quoting that philosophy crap to me!" Katrina sidled close to Alexandra. "I'm with you, I bet he's a real dweeb."

"At least he's real. You two should stop talking about the perfect man and go out and find one. Maybe tonight, if you can stop criticizing my boyfriend long enough to look." Kate walked ahead of them, the sound of her heels lost in the grind of bus wheels in Taylor Square.

"Humourless bitch." Katrina muttered.

Kate turned into a stairwell on her left and called out to them. "Paradise within. Or Hades, depends on your spiritual compass." She ascended the stairs.

Alexandra peered upwards and caught the shimmer of Kate's vintage dress in the half-light. A pulsating beat vibrated in the stairwell. The silver line of Kate's heels beckoned them on.

"Patronizing bitch." Katrina looked up. "This looks like a gay bar."

An aroma of mould and cigarettes pervaded as they climbed the stairs. They entered a long, low-ceiling lounge area. Intimate nooks of dark brown sofas were scattered near a black leather bar. Fit men stood in clusters, their drinks held in tanned hands. In the corner of the room, a dance floor was packed with bodies. A neon strobe threw a psychedelic sheen on the dancers.

"It's a gay bar." Katrina looked down at her striped jumpsuit. "And I look like Princess Di. It's OK for Kate to lecture us on men but we're not exactly gonna meet anyone tonight."

"Don't worry, no one can see what you're wearing. It's too dark." Alexandra motioned to the bar. "Let's get a drink and sit somewhere. At least we don't have to worry about getting hit on. And we can always talk to her Billy."

"Great, we have her loincloth for company. I can see this'll be a memorable night, right up there with a baked dinner at my aunt's house."

They pushed towards the crowded bar as the sexy voice of George Michael sounded on the speakers. "Let's dance, we'll never make it to the bar." Katrina pointed to an empty sofa. "Leave your bag there."

"Hope I see it again." Alexandra shouted in Katrina's ear and she shouted back.

"You will, the only thing they'd nick is your makeup." She tugged her arm. "C'mon, they're playing Culture Club, my fav."

Alexandra relaxed, let the tribal call of her generation enter her body. She loved to dance, she felt her body become light with music. She waved at Kate nearby, arms encircled around the shoulders of a brown haired boy. He looked up briefly, then focused on the surrendering body of Kate.

Freedom welled within Alexandra. She watched the crowd, sensing rhythm in some. A tall, handsome boy jostled closer and danced with her. Katrina peeled off into the crowd. Alexandra danced with her unknown partner, the London songs vivid in her blood. The song changed, a fifties love song created an intimate mood. The boy held out his hand and she hesitated, then moved closer to his pliant body.

"This is bliss." She thought as he held her. They moved in a waltz pattern, their bodies in sync. The unknown boy smiled again and the muscle underneath his shirt caught Alexandra's senses sharply.

The mood changed again as a nostalgic tune of the Beatles played next on the speakers. The boy nodded to her and vanished into the crowd. Alexandra still felt his touch on her skin as she walked back to the sofa.

"Glad you're back." Katrina shouted over the music. "I still feel like an absolute dickhead in these clothes." She passed her a drink. "Gin for you. Where'd the gorgeous boy go?"

"Probably off kissing his boyfriend."

"Did you ask him?"

"No."

"Wasted opportunity, fine looking specimen. You should have talked to him."

"He's not gonna be interested in me. And I never speak to men unless I establish their sexuality first. And he's definitely sexually ambiguous!"

"At least you got a dance, unlike wallflower me."

Kate approached the sofa, holding hands with a sweet-faced boy. "Bill, you remember Alexandra. You met her last week. And this is Katrina."

Katrina raised her glass. "Cheers. I'd have got one for you, Kate, but I don't know what you drink."

Kate stood. "That's ok. Bourbon for you, Bill?"

He nodded and she headed to the bar.

"So you finish economics at the end of the year." Katrina leaned forward. "What'll you do when you graduate?"

"I hope to be in England early next year, working in London."

"With Kate?"

He shrugged his shoulders. "I don't think she'll finish her degree anytime soon." His smile highlighted lines that fanned from his eyes to his cheeks. It added to his boyishness and Alexandra felt an inexplicable pang. He looked across at her.

"Your folks don't mind you going out on Christmas Eve? Kate said they were really strict."

"I said I was going to the movies with Katrina."

"I'm your excuse? At least I'm good for something tonight."

Alexandra grinned at Bill. "She's mad with Kate that we're at a gay bar."

"What about you?"

"It's kinda entertaining. These boys know how to dance."

"Want to?" Bill stood and held out a hand to her. "She'll be ages at the bar."

Katrina pushed her. "Go on. You don't want to become a professional wallflower, like me."

"Bliss again in the arms of another safe boy." Alexandra thought. "And he knows how to dance." She surrendered to his movement as the London song blared out. A Bill Haley song played next and he jived her into his arms. She swung and followed his lead. Sweat and aftershave hung in the air and she felt light-headed. Under the neon light, she glimpsed Kate's nonplussed face as she balanced drinks in her hands, walking back from the bar.

Alexandra shouted in Bill's ear. "Kate's got your drink, we should sit down."

"She's moody tonight. She can stay on her own for a bit." A seventies disco song started. "I can't dance to this shit."

"I agree. Good to see you've got musical taste. C'mon, let's head back." She shook his arm off as he tried to pull her back. "Please." She pleaded. "Kate's unhappy, I can tell."

"So what? She's not your problem."

She crossed the floor quickly. She looked behind to see if he followed her and saw him approach another girl to dance. The girl smiled and took his hand. Alexandra turned away.

Kate sat, legs crossed and cigarette in hand as Bill finally approached the sofa. "Your ice melted."

He kissed the top of her head. "We should do this again, it's a good place."

Katrina whispered to Alexandra. "Kate's pissed off with you."

"Why?"

"For having a good time with him."

"Obviously she's not."

"And if she can't, no one else can. You know what she's like."

Alexandra watched Kate and Bill in deep discussion.

He leaned forward to Katrina and Alexandra. "We're gonna move on to Rogue's nightclub. Will you come?"

Kate interrupted. "Actually, I won't, Bill. I don't want too late a night. I'll call you tomorrow." She stood and pulled Alexandra upwards. "Let's dance, I love this song." She blew him a kiss as she walked away.

He stared, then left without another word.

Katrina spoke aloud to herself. "I must be invisible in these clothes." She raised her glass in the air. "Goodnight Bill, nice to meet you."

Alexandra followed Kate, the pulsating dance floor a blur to her. Her heart beat rapidly as she watched Kate move to the music.

"Let's go," Kate pulled her close. "These queens aggravate me."

Alexandra collected her bag as they moved through the crush to the exit.

"Never again, Kate," Katrina spoke as they stood on the pavement outside the nightclub, "are you gonna pick the club we go to."

"You'd have picked Newtown RSL if I left it to you."

"At least I'd have had the chance to dance with one heterosexual male if we went there. I couldn't ask Billy to dance, could I? You would've had a pink fit if we both danced with him."

Alexandra looked at Kate but she remained silent.

Katrina flagged down an approaching bus and turned to Alexandra. "I'm getting this one home. Wanna come?"

"I'll get the next one to Central. See ya at Uni."

Katrina averted her eyes from Kate as she walked away.

Abruptly, Kate linked arms with Alexandra. "Let's walk through Hyde Park for a bit. The wind can blow the cigarette smoke off me. Mother doesn't know I smoke."

"She can't be that thick."

"She's naive."

A harbour wind buffeted the War Memorial. A nesting bird called out from a tree and the sound echoed in the open space.

They walked past the reflecting pond, as moonlight shone into its shallow depths.

Alexandra spoke. "Do you want to drop by St Mary's Cathedral? We might catch the last part of Midnight mass."

"You really go for that ceremonial stuff, don't you? Catholic atonement of sin. Wash the Taylor Square debauchery off you."

"Kate!" Alexandra eyes filled with tears. "Are you pissed off that I danced with Bill? Just say it."

"He can dance with anyone, I don't care." Kate flicked her hair from her shoulders and it gleamed dark gold under the park lamps. "We don't see each other much, just on weekends. If he can't make time for me, that's his problem."

"You were at the bar."

"Forget it, it's not important." Kate whispered. "He's not important." She stopped in front of the Cathedral and looked up. Floodlights shone skywards and created dramatic shadows on the facade. On the stairs to the side entrance, a disparate collection of women sat together, soothing tired babies and toddlers.

Kate pulled Christmas ornaments from her handbag and handed them to Alexandra. "I nicked them from the bar while I was waiting to be served. I'm gonna wear mine now, so I can look festive for Jesus."
Alexandra attached hers to her necklace. "Thanks. I've never had a stolen Christmas present before."
They entered the Cathedral and slipped into a pew amongst the packed congregation. Jesus hung on the cross over the altar, welcomed the visitors with bowed head. Tourists welded Nikon cameras. Flash bulbs sparked intermittently.
Alexandra made the sign of the cross.
"More mysterious ceremony." Kate whispered.
Incense hung in the humid air. Richly costumed old men trailed past, the colours of ritual woven into their vestments. Choirboys began a hymn and the church resonated with song. Each pure note seemed to seep into the sandstone walls.
"This is quite a show." Kate whispered.
Alexandra nodded, lightheaded by incense and alcohol as the congregation stood for the final hymn. Weary children lay cradled in their parents' arms. The soaring notes reverberated inside the cathedral, then faded away.

They exited the Cathedral in silence and walked through Hyde Park. Street lamps lit the sultry night and they idled in front of the David Jones window display.
"The pagan conquest of Christmas." Kate murmured. "What do you do on the day?"
Alexandra answered. "It's a big celebration. Ma's in her element, all her friends come for dinner and get tipsy on Dad's wine. They sing after lunch, all the old songs of their village and Ma cries. Pina and I escape inside to wash up. Pretty sad, huh?"

"More interesting than my day." Kate slipped her heels off and walked barefoot on the grass. "Mother cooks a turkey for lunch and then complains how inappropriate it feels to bake for just the two of us and how strange it is to eat a roast in hot weather. Some rellos we only ever see at Christmas come over for afternoon tea and make small talk about excruciatingly boring things."

Couples sauntered past them. Within Alexandra, the same pang at the sight of love.

"I'll get this bus." Kate spoke. "You'll be OK here?"

"Yeah. Kate...."

Too late. She had moved out of hearing distance. Kate called out from her window as the bus began to pull out. "Watch out for the man in red, I hears he likes Italian chicks."

Alexandra waved goodbye. Her eyes followed the gleam of Kate's silver dress as it vanished from her sight. She remembered the touch of handsomeness bequeathed to her by dance. She looked at the crowds that passed her, on their way to clubs and bars, as she flagged her bus. It took her back to suburbia.

Chapter 11

Alexandra leaned against the railing and breathed in. "I love this time of year, Beth. The air's so invigorating."

The older woman shivered. She tucked loose strands of red hair into her cap as she replied.

"You won't say that in another twenty years, my dear. These cold snaps aggravate my arthritis." She jumped up and down on the spot. "I don't know why it takes Roger so long to get our walks started. He uses the same checklist every Sunday." She stared at the sprightly man navigating between the group of bush walkers.

He called out from a checklist and ticked off items as he walked.

Alexandra replied. "Poor Roger, I think he's a frustrated CEO at heart. He probably wishes we were at the Himalayan base camp now, instead of a humble Blue Mountains trek."

"He's a control freak. My first husband was the same."

"Was that the husband that left you for his secretary? "

"No, that was husband number two." She tapped Alexandra's arm. "Got a first husband in your closet?"

"No, I'm not that interesting."

"Come close?"

"No."

Alexandra looked at her walking group. A disparate collection of middle-aged people, they had walked through milestones together: death, divorce, marriage, birth, bankruptcy and retrenchment. Words unsaid, as they kept apace of each other.

"I've been saved by their unsaid words," she mused, "many times."

She turned back to Beth. "Roger's going overboard this time. Wentworth Falls hardly registers as a remote walking track. I don't think we need a compass and first aid kit."

"Remote my foot!" Beth stretched her legs. "We bump into a thousand tourists on the climb down. We're not even out of mobile range." She nudged Alexandra. "That bloke's calling out to you."

Alexandra looked across. "I don't believe it, I never thought he'd come!"

Beth's eyes sparkled as she murmured. "I do love a mystery." She watched as Alexandra sprang forward to greet the man.

"Frank!" She looked him up and down. "Did you buy those clothes yesterday? You look like a walking billboard for Nike."

"Don't give me a hard time. I feel stupid enough already." He tugged his track pants and shuffled his pristine runners in the dirt track.

Beth nudged her. "Introduction, please."

"Beth, this is my manager, Frank. He's the bloke I've invited to join our group."

"Good to have you here today. I'll let Roger know we've got a new walker." She winked at Alexandra as she passed by. "Closet's not so empty now, is it?"

"What'd she say?" Frank leaned against the railing and stretched out his feet. "Bloody shoes are killing me. Sales assistant told me I'd feel like I was walking on air. The liar. How long does the walk go for?"

"About three hours."

"Shit."

"When was the last time you walked?"

He frowned in concentration. "Uni?"

"Oh dear. Maybe we won't go all the way down today, some of the ladders are pretty hard."

"Ladders? We're going on a walking track."

"Some of it's down sheer cliffs. That's when we use the ladders."

"You didn't mention you bloody abseil on these walks. I knew these people would be mad. Alexy, I can't go down ladders, I get...."

Alexandra lifted her eyebrow to silence him as a short, lean man approached them.

"G'day, mate. Beth tells me you're a friend of Alex. I'm Roger." He extended his sinewy hand and shook Frank's with a hard grip.

"Good to meet you, Captain. Yeah, Alexy's nagged me for years to do this."

"I didn't! I merely suggested it."

Roger interrupted them. "Good on you, Mate. It's never too late to get fit. You'll find the kilos will roll off and your fitness levels will improve dramatically. This is a tough walk to start on but we'll look after you." He eyed Frank's shape. "Alex, we won't give him anything to carry today, he's carrying enough." He moved away.

Frank looked after him. "I think he knows my brother-in-law. Same insults directed in same innocent fashion."

"Roger's OK. Now look at the beautiful valley below you and breathe the fresh air into your lungs."

"If they don't explode first."

Roger signaled to the group. "Let's start. Frank, mate, walk alongside me and I'll explain the history of the group to you."

Frank bent to Alexandra. "How old's the Captain?"

"I think he's sixty five."

"Brilliant, fifteen years older than me. I can't back out now." He looked at the soles of his sandshoes. "I hope they've got grip, otherwise you're carrying me down."

Beth walked past them and winked again at Alexandra.

"She thinks you fancy me." Alexandra murmured.

"That's not what I'm thinking now." Sweat stood on his forehead as he moved forward to walk alongside Roger. Alexandra watched as Frank tried to keep up with Roger's half-jogging step.

He removed his long sleeve top and tied it around his waist.

Roger eyed his girth as Frank straightened up. After ten minutes, he stopped and paused on a step. "Captain, I'm gonna admire the view and wait for Alexy. I want to thank her for inviting me today."

"Take five minutes out, mate. You look pasty, don't want to overdo it on your first walk." Roger slapped his back and continued jogging down the step path.

Alexandra waited till the group passed by and stood beside him as he caught his breath.

Frank stared at the valley beneath them, the only sound the screech of black cockatoos as they flew over. He picked at the lint collecting on his track pants as he finally spoke. "I'm dying and that bastard knows it."

She remained silent.

"I didn't bring lunch, I thought we'd go to a café in Leura."

"It's only 10am. Anyway, you can share my sandwich. If you make it down to the valley, that is."

"I hate you." Frank waved his hand towards the valley. "But I know why you do this. I'm boxed into a boring suburban routine, I wash my car and water my garden every weekend and for what?"

"Don't wax too philosophical, Frank. Give it another hour."

"I may not be capable of speech then. Hear me now."

She laughed. "C'mon, keep walking but go slow. I don't want you to die on my shift."

"You're not related to Roger, are you?"

A bird sailed past, its wings propelled by air pockets. Alexandra gazed at the valley.

"You want me to shut up, don't you?"

"No, I was just thinking that this is my only quiet time. My week is scheduled. Here, I'm able to think. Except if you're around!"

"Touché. How are you coping with sharing your flat?"

"I don't see Kate much, she's always with her daughter. One thing annoyed me though; she hung an icon on my wall as a present. She reads me like there's a one sentence explanation of my character: religious, old maid."

"You mean you're really a dark horse?"

"Shut up! I don't like being summarized. She did it all the time at Uni."

"Why'd you put up with it? Blokes just tell each other to fuck off."

"That's why the world's such a mess now, too many men in power." She stared at the valley. "We weren't raised to be assertive kids. I never knew how to stand my ground."

"Tell her to move out, that you've had enough of her freeloading."

"This conversation is so Mars and Venus."

"I had a cousin from England come out last year and he stayed four nights. I nearly killed him, he was a total pig. He went across to WA, then wanted to stay another week with me. I told him I'd rented the room out."

"I couldn't lie like that, my conscience would kill me."

"You would if you saw the mess he made."

"Well, I'm taking the icon down."

They had descended into a small, fern-filled valley. Roger motioned for the group to rest. They sat down on mossy rocks and Alexandra offered her drink bottle to Frank.

"Thanks. How long does the Captain let us rest?"

"Five minutes."

"He's gotta be ex-army."

"Close, ex-army reserves."

"God help me." He looked at the group. "It's like you're a bunch of monks, on a spiritual retreat from the world and Roger's the Abbot."

"I'd never thought of it that way."

"See, I can summarize and insult you in a sentence too."

"Don't forget I've got the food supplies."

He grinned.

Alexandra turned her face to the sun, as a brackish scent pervaded the air. "I'll talk to her," she decided. "So she knows the boundaries."

Birdcalls sounded in the valley below as she stretched out.

"Let's go." Roger's voice boomed out.

"The fun bit's coming up, Frank. We'll walk behind the others."

He was silent as they walked around a rock crevice that circled a small waterfall.

"Be careful here. It's slippery."

"I'm fat, not stupid, Alexy."

The group waited at the edge of a cliff as Roger called out. "Let's start the descent, we'll have lunch at the base." He turned and nimbly descended a ladder, embedded into the rock face.

Frank licked his lips as they waited at the back of the line. "I can't do it." He whispered.

She stared at him.

"I can't stand heights, I get vertigo."

"It's really safe," she whispered back. "They're steel ladders with a protective brace so you can't fall outwards, just down."

"Oh I feel much better, thank you. They could have bloody Sir Edmund Hillary strapped to my waist, God rest his soul, and I couldn't do it."

She caught Beth staring at them as she descended the ladder ahead of them. "She's convinced you're whispering sweet nothings in my ear."

"Nothing further from my mind, I could kill you for getting me into this situation."

"Oh please! I didn't drag you here with a rope."

They watched as the last of the group descended and continued their walk below.

"We'll go slow, Beth." Alexandra called out. "Meet you at the base."

The older woman gave a sly smile as she waved at them.

"They're gone." Alexandra turned to him. "Now what?"

Frank leaned back and allowed a couple to pass him. They looked Northern European; blonde, fit and tanned. "He's got a stitch," Alexandra addressed them. "Gets them all the time."

They gave a sympathetic smile as they passed.

"I thought you said you couldn't lie." Frank muttered. "Sounded professional to me."

"I was saving your male pride." She tapped her foot. "I don't know why I bothered." She moved across to the first rung on the ladder.

"Just give it a go. Put your foot on the first step and see how you feel. I'll stand beneath you and we'll go down as far as you can."

He wiped his forehead.

She came back and took his hand. "Every little step is an achievement."

"Piss off, Alexy. Save that motivational stuff for the staff." He bit his lip. "Sorry. You go on, I'll head back and have lunch somewhere."

"You drove all this way! I'll call Roger tonight and tell him you punctured a lung, he'll understand that. C'mon, I know a great café at Leura."

"Thanks."

"Don't think you're getting out of exercise completely. We'll walk around the village after lunch."

"Aye, aye, Captain." He tugged her hair as they turned back.

1972: Tilli Panna

The heat rose from the concrete path and seeped into her thongs. The wheels on the trolley beside her made a squeaky sound and Alexandra watched as they turned on their small axis.

"I'm tired, Mama. Why can't you take Pina to the shops? She always gets to stay home."

"Because she likes shopping. You need to learn to shop, cara mia, so you can look after your family when you grow up."

"I won't have one, so I don't need to learn."

"Everyone should have a family. Life is empty without one."

"Did you feel empty before you had me?"

"Yes."

Alexandra glanced at her mother as she pushed the shopping trolley. She wore a yellow shift dress and Roman sandals. Cat glasses sat on her hooked nose and her hair was caught in a bun at the nap of her neck. An ornate brooch was clipped to one side of her dress. The treeless street they walked along was lined on either side with single storey, fibro houses. Low, grey bushes dotted sparse lawns. The air itself seemed to wither in the heat. Claudia walked at a brisk pace. Behind them, a tinkling bell sounded and Alexandra turned back. A boy approached on his bike, peddling at a desultory rate.

"Careful, Alexandra! Move to the side." Her mother pulled her onto the grass as the boy slowly overtook them. "Move to the inside, cara, so the cars aren't near you."

Alexandra moved across.

"Tilli Pana." Her mother murmured as she watched the boy cycle away in the hazy glare.

"What does that mean? You always say that when we see a bicycle."

"You listen too much to old people."

"You're not old. Please tell me what it means."

Claudia smiled.

"It's the secret," thought Alexandra "it's here again!"

"Tilli Pana was a man who lived in my village."

"Did you know him?"

"No, I was a child when he was an old man. He had no family left, his sons died in the war." She looked away as she continued on. "He lived in a barn on a farmer's land. The farmer let him stay there with his cows because he was poor and alone." Claudia's hand began to shake as she spoke and Alexandra watched her grip the trolley firmly. Her knuckles stood out in the blinding light.

"It's spring in my village now, the flowers are in the fields and growing high in the mountains. The snow is gone and the cuckoo have returned to sing in the forest. My sisters and I would walk to collect beautiful flowers for Mama, to bring spring to her kitchen."

"Why didn't she walk with you?"

"She had no time, she had five children to cook and sew for."

"What didn't she buy food at the shops? Then she would have time."

Claudia smiled. "There were no shops in my village. We ate what we grew or could buy from neighbours' farms."

Alexandra walked alongside her mother.

"We would walk near the railway line. On Saturdays, the steam train would come to our village, to bring the men home from the city, to see their families. We could see the smoke rising from high in the mountain and we would run to the station."

"Did your cousin come too, the boy made of gold?"

"Sometimes." Claudia's eyes crinkled, a curved line fanned out from her eyelids and seemed to trap her expression in a permanent smile. "Roland, he would jump on the train as it came down the mountain and smoke cigarettes with the men inside. He would pretend I am his girlfriend when the train arrive at the station and give me a big kiss and tell me how much he miss me all week, away working. Everyone would laugh because they knew he tell a lie."

Alexandra stared at Claudia's face. It was animated in tender warmth, with a light she never saw in her eyes when she spoke to Emilio.

"But what about Tilli Pana?"

"Sometimes we would see him, as we walk near the train tracks. He was very old and had lost his ears...." Claudia paused. "How you say this, Alexandra?"

"Deaf, he couldn't hear."

"Brava, he was deaf. He walked his cows on the tracks, because the grass was good along there and didn't belong to any farms. One of the cows wore a little bell, that rang in the wind."

"Wasn't it dangerous to walk on the tracks if he was deaf?"

"Tilli Pana could feel the train coming from many miles away, with his feet, the...."

"Vibrations."

"Si! And he would call the cows to the side until the train passed by."

"Clever Tilli Pana."

"He was." She looked ahead as she spoke. "He would call to the cows, like a song; tilli, tilli, tilli, tilli pana. We never knew his real name, we called him Tilli Pana, after the song."

"Did you ever talk to him?"

"No, we hid behind trees and watch him pass by. If he saw anyone, he would be ashamed because he was too poor to own his own field. Mama said never to shame a poor man, it was a sin."

"He's dead now?"

Claudia nodded.

"What happened to his cows when he died?"

Her mother made the sign of the cross before she spoke. "They all died the day he did."

Alexandra stopped walking.

"He had to walk his cows in the rain or the sun. He was sick that spring, they say he had pneumonia on the lungs and couldn't feel anything with his feet because he was so sick. He walked on the tracks that day, searching for the best grass. The train hit him first, then destroyed all the cows. The train driver had a heart attack in the shock but he lived. He said the last thing he would see before he died was Tilli Pana walking his cows."

Claudia ruffled Alexandra's hair. "You need to be careful in life, cara mia. It's full of sadness if you are not." She quickened her pace and they walked in silence the rest of the way. Another bicycle bell tinkled in the heat and Claudia pulled Alexandra onto the grass again. The bike sped away and they continued their walk.

"I know some of her secrets now," Alexandra thought proudly. "I'm special."

Chapter 12

Kate examined them. Isabella sat beside Rosemary, her hand resting on her grandmother's arm. Rosemary stroked it as she listened. "I called Dad last night. He said the new bathroom looks so good, it's a shame to use it. And he's pulled the old bulbs out and bought some new soil. I'm planting bulbs when we get back."

"I hope grandma didn't mind you using her phone."

"I told her to."

Kate stared out the café window at the import shops, Vietnamese bread shops and fruit and veg shops. The elderly, sullen teenagers and migrants jostled together in a swell of human traffic along the pavement. She stared at a shaft of sunlight that fell between two shops and lit the concrete path in a halo of light. People passed through the light, briefly illuminated, then continued to walk under the dark awnings.

"What is it, dear? Are you thinking of Nicholas?"

Kate glanced at her mother.

"It's alright. Isabella and I have discussed it at length. It's best to be forthright with children, they need to understand as much as we do."

"Have you spoken to Dad this week?"

"No."

"Well, he said he's counting the days till I get back. Everyone's asking me on Facebook when I get back. Since Grandma doesn't have a computer, we go to an internet café after lunch."

Kate raised her eyebrows. "That's so 21st century, Mother!"

"It's fun. Isabella has taught me how to surf the net."

"Unbelievable, Bella! You've performed a miracle."

Isabella squeezed Rosemary's arm and Kate stared at the gesture.

"Have you done more gardening?"

"Lots, we've planted tons of bulbs. It's a shame I won't see them in flower but Grandma said she'd take lots of photos."

"Perhaps you will."

"What do you mean?"

"We've got open tickets, so we can stay longer."

"But I'm already missing school term, I don't want to lose any more. Ruby said we're doing lots of new maths. I'll have so much to catch up on." She looked away. "When do we go home?" she whispered.

"I'm not sure, Bella. We'll see."

"What do you mean?" Isabella raised her voice. "Can't you just say when? You never give a direct answer to anything."

"That's not true." Kate licked her lips and saw Rosemary's eyes focus on the gesture. "There's a few variables at the moment. Nicholas is renovating and we'd just get in the way."

"I don't believe you."

"Can we talk about this privately?"

"We can talk in front of Grandma. You don't have to be so secretive. Dad hates it too."

"That's enough, you're starting to attract stares. Let's leave it for now."

Isabella was silent.

"It's the best hot chocolate this side of the Harbour Bridge." Rosemary drained her mug. "I've been coming here for years."

"It's delicious. Did you come here with Grandpa?"

"No, on my own. I'd stop and have a cup after I did my grocery shopping."

"Did Mum come?"

"Kate was always in a hurry to be somewhere as a teenager. She had to see the latest film, read the latest book, or see the newest exhibition at the Art Gallery. She had no time to be with her boring mother. It's the same with every generation."

"True. Bella would rather garden than come with me to Newtown."

They eyed each other in silence.

"What was Grandpa like? Mum never talks about him."

Kate whispered. "He was a poet."

Rosemary leaned forward. "A what? Kate, you were always fanciful. I thought you would outgrow that by now." She turned to Isabella. "He wasn't, dear. He was an Engineer. A fine one too, trained in London. He worked in the same firm in Sydney for twenty years. Not like today, where five years in a company is considered long service. No, Hugh was from the generation that understood that stability was integral to a man's reputation."

Kate half-closed her eyes as she spoke. "He believed in fairies and magic. I believed in them too, when he was alive."

"Nonsense," Rosemary interjected. "You can't summarize him like that, makes him sound superficial. He was a fine man."

"You can be fine and lyrical too. He was."

"Your lyrical nature didn't get you far, didn't even finish your degree. That's the problem with today's generation, no ability to apply themselves."

Kate stared out the window again. "Strathfield hasn't changed much." She murmured.

"Speak up, Kate. It's hard to hear you." Rosemary leaned forward. "And don't you believe it, prices have soared in the inner west. I don't know how a young couple could afford a home in Sydney now, let alone educate their children decently. You were lucky your father had a good job and could afford a private school. The rubbish they teach at public schools is deplorable. Thank heavens Isabella is at a good school."

"Indeed."

Kate sat back as they chattered together. Their practical talk was foreign to her. Isabella's eyes were alight with interest as they discussed her school and friends in London.

Kate watched passers by as she listened.

"Did Grandpa like gardening?"

She started back to the present as Rosemary replied. "Hated it. He'd spend hours in the garage constructing Meccano sets with Kate. They made the most amazing towers and buildings, then they would play with them for hours. He was very patient with her. I would feel quite lonely, with the two of them always busy."

"Dad makes me read when I stay with him. He says that words are the most evocative tool of memory."

Kate looked across at Isabella. "Did Nicholas say that?"

"He says it all the time." Isabella pushed her fringe impatiently out of her eyes. "Can we go to Bondi tomorrow?"

"We're going to town tomorrow. There's an exhibition of Frederick McCubben paintings at the Gallery. We can have a picnic lunch at Lady Macquarie's Chair after."

"We do that boring stuff in London!"

Kate leaned forward. "They're enormously important paintings. The beginning of an Australian consciousness, like impressionism re-invented for the bush. You'll love it."

Rosemary nudged Isabella. "What would you rather do?"

"Go to Bondi markets. I bought shell earrings last week, I want to get my girlfriends some before we go home. If Mum can make up her mind when we're going." She avoided Kate's eyes.

Rosemary nodded to Kate. "She needs stability. It's about time you provided some." She stood stiffly and walked to the counter. "My treat."

Chapter 13: Faulconbridge, 1983 Norman Lindsay's House

"He loved tits."

"That's your summary of his artistic career?" Kate stared at Alexandra.

"Succinct if you ask me." Katrina walked behind them. "Norman Lindsay was a dirty old man, obsessed with voluptuous handmaidens flirting with demons in Hades." She followed them onto the verandah. "OK, we've done the artistic bit. Let's eat. Did your ma make lunch, Alex?"

"Is the Pope Jewish? Let's sit on the grass somewhere. Don't look so glum, Kate. Sometimes you have to slum it with plebs in the art world."

Kate followed behind them as they made their way to the lawn of Lindsay's cottage.

Katrina walked across to a fountain and whistled. "Check out the upright boobs on this one! He definitely didn't like middle-aged chicks."

They sat on the lawn. The garden was a rich palette of summer hues, the artist's vision of the grounds clearly defined. Gum trees provided a subtle backdrop to European plantings. Roman columns and classical fountains merged into the bush landscape.

"I would've loved to have met him." Kate murmured.

Alexandra unwrapped sandwiches from her backpack. "You were just his type, too."

Kate lifted her face to the sun and closed her eyes. Her hair cascaded behind her back in thick, blonde waves. "It's so peaceful. I understand how he could work here."

"It's got a sleepy aura to it." Katrina looked about. "I imagine him lying in a hammock, throwing crumbs to stray wallabies, being fanned by naked nymphs."

"How kinky of you." Alexandra grinned. "I don't think he was idle much. Too much testosterone and ambition."

"Short guys seem to have it in inverse proportion to their body height."

"Are you speaking from worldly experience, Kit Kat?"

"Just trying to sound sophisticated. Pathetic, I know."

"Totally. Kate's the one to ask."

"You flatter me." Kate held up her sandwich. "What's in this? It weighs a ton."

"That's my Italian ma for you. She includes all the ingredients of the food pyramid in one humble sandwich. That's why I'm getting so fat."

"All European chicks have hips." Katrina replied. "Makes having babies easier. Apparently."

Kate lifted her sketchpad out of her bag and stared at Alexandra.

"Don't even think about it! I look such a dag."

"I've wanted to sketch you for ages. Please, it won't take long. This is the perfect place to play muse. Don't move!"

Alexandra pulled a book out of her bag. "I'm gonna read while you draw."

"Perfect, it'll help my interpretation of your character."

Katrina lay down on the grass. "I'm having a siesta. Good luck, Alex."

Kate ignored her as she held her charcoal pencil to her lips. "What are you reading?"

"Jane Eyre. I found an old copy last week, at Newtown." Alexandra held the book against her drawn knees.

"Perfect," Kate set her pad on her lap. "Jane, Jane, Jane! Where are you?"

"You're making fun of me."

"No, it's one of the most romantic books in English literature."

"I know. I can't decide which I love best: Jane Eyre or Wuthering Heights."

Katrina cocked an eye open. "The Bronte chicks were psychos. I could never get into their books, the protagonists were so bloody tortured. I bet Jane Eyre rued the day she married Rochester."

"Rubbish," Alexandra's cheeks flushed as she spoke. "They were kindred spirits, as essential to each other as air and water."

"Give me a well-adjusted bloke anytime."

"Like Tom?" Kate glanced at Katrina. "If he were any more meat and potatoes, you could bake him."

"What's wrong with that? At least he's reliable. He won't piss off to London like Bill did, with flowery promises to write." Katrina closed her eyes and turned her back on Kate.

Alexandra read the vivid dialogue of Miss Bronte as Kate sketched her.

The sun rose higher in the sky as bird calls punctured the silence. Kate glanced at the bush surrounding them.

"It's almost McCubbenesque," she thought as she sketched the tree line, rubbing her charcoal to soften the lines of the landscape.

Alexandra closed her book. "That was gorgeous." She rested her head on her knees.

"And so are you." Kate handed her the pad.

"Oh!" Alexandra stared at the fine, charcoal strokes.

"I can see you like it." Kate smiled. "I think it's good too."

Katrina sat up. "Show me." She examined the sketch. "You can draw! I thought you were bull-shitting us, like usual."

"You're the only person I know that can turn a compliment into an insult. Apart from my mother." Kate continued. "Alexandra translates well in charcoal, it's easy to capture her romantic dreaminess."

Alexandra placed the book into her bag. "I'm not dreamy. No-one's ever said that before."

"But you are, underneath the pragmatic front lies a Bronte heartbeat. I watched you read. As you got to the end chapter, you inched closer to the pages. You were Jane Eyre. We've got to find you a Rochester, you deserve nothing less."

"She deserves a lot more."

"No, you're wrong." Kate pulled her knees up. "Alexandra needs someone who'll love her passionately." She pulled at blades of grass as she spoke to Alexandra. "How's the Engineer? Have you progressed beyond coffee at Uni?"

"Never will. Nick's the golden boy, he's got a brilliant career ahead of him. We're just mates."

"That's not what he told me. He'd love to go out with you."

"Rubbish! He's never said that to me."

"You don't let him."

"He's free to speak."

"No, he's not." Kate brushed stray grass clippings off her pad. "You steer the conversation away from all that. He's got no chance to be personal because you're too controlling."

Katrina rose to her knees. "Shut up, psychology queen of 1983. You can't keep a guy for more than six months. They get sick of your minute analysis of their defects."

"There's no need to turn on me. I'm not much of a friend if I can't say what I think. I've known Alexandra for two years and it's always the same excuse. He's too gorgeous or too intelligent or she's too woggy for him."

"It's rubbish." Alexandra stretched her legs. "Nick can say anything he wants."

"Anything you want to hear," Kate continued. "You analyze people as outside of your field of experience and then, never experience anything. Pragmatic to the point of being self- destructive." She ran her hands over her knees. "You should take a risk, dream a little." She spoke softly. "A life lived in fear is a life half lived."

Alexandra turned away abruptly.

"Shut up with that bloody philosopher!" Katrina mouthed silently to Kate.

"It's your turn, Kit Kat." Kate smiled. "Stretch out, lean your head on your hands and tilt your face to the sun. That position suits you."

"Oh please, does my portrait come with free psychoanalysis too?"

"Only if you need it. And you don't. Now, keep still."

Alexandra lay on her stomach. Her black hair fell forward, the pattern of coarse hairs blurred her vision and shielded her face.

"War words," she thought, "how could she use them on me?" The air seemed too still for the tumult within her heart.

"You OK, Alex? I'll punch her if you want me to."

"I'm absolutely fine." Alexandra answered Katrina, as she lifted her head. "I'm just dreaming of Mr Rochester."

She laid her head on her interlaced hands. The bitter words of her childhood played in her memory. Control was necessary in the war house. She remembered her parents faces as they screamed at each other, homesickness their hidden dialogue. When exhausted with words, they would hate each other silently. Tears threatened as she lay still, the sun warm on her back.

The only sounds were the call of native birds and Kate's pencil on the sketchpad.

Alexandra breathed deeply.

"What do you think?" Kate held up her sketch.

Alexandra sat upright, blinking in the sunlight. "It's excellent! You've really captured her expression."

Katrina looked over her shoulder. "I look pretty. Thanks, Kate."

"You're welcome. You can give it to meat and potato boy. Maybe he'll sleep with it under his pillow."

"Very funny."

Kate packed away her pencils and glanced at Alexandra. "I capture the emotional pretty well too. I don't take back what I said. Take a little risk sometimes."

"That's enough free counselling for today." Katrina interrupted her. "We should head to Katoomba and have a hot chocolate somewhere." She gave a droll look. "If we survive my driving skills. Watch out, Kate. The annoying passengers are always the first to go in a collision."

They walked in silence to the car. The sky seemed darker to Alexandra, as if a cloak had covered the serene blue in a deeper hue.

Chapter 14

"Frank, get your big feet off my desk."

He ignored her request and stretched out his legs. "It's seven pm on a Friday night, Alexy. What are we still doing at work?"

"End of month financial crap for our clients. What a pair of tragics!"

He was silent.

"You walking this Sunday?"

"Yeah. They're a good bunch of bastards. Even Roger."

"Beth's convinced we're having an affair. As are the girls in the branch."

He remained serious. "I feel like having an affair. Why don't we?"

"Frank, you're my boss. Quit your job and then we'll talk."

"You've always got an answer. Bet you've put off heaps of guys with that."

"Not as many as you think."

"I've known you seven years but I don't know much about you. Ever been in love, Alexy? No smart reply please."

She didn't know where to place her arms on the desk. Somehow, the motion seemed important.

"Once."

"Love or lust?"

"Both, but mostly love."

"And he didn't marry you. Stupid bastard."

"I only knew him for six weeks. I met him on holidays in England."

"You tart."

She was silent.

"Now we're both in a morbid mood." Frank twined his hands behind his head. "I have an outwardly successful life; a good job, great place. I should be content but mostly, I feel like crap."

"Mid-life crisis has hit you, Frank."

"I said no jokes."

"I wasn't. I went through it when I turned forty. Do you know the 'Far Side' cards? I got one for my birthday years ago. It had a screaming woman on the cover. The inside caption read: 'I'm forty! Oh my God, I forgot to have children!' That's how I felt that day, like I forgot to do the things I really wanted or I wasn't brave enough to do."

"Hey, when I said no jokes, I didn't mean make me cry."
"You don't have the monopoly on when people can be serious or funny."
"Touché."
"How about you, even been in love?"
"Twice. I was engaged once but it never panned out."
"What happened?"
"She was too possessive. I stopped seeing her and she got the message. She rang me one day, abusing me. Told me I could shove the engagement ring into a dark region of my body that I won't mention in polite company."
She laughed. "You should've been more up-front with her."
"If I wasn't so scared of her, sure." He paused. "So, what happened to the English bloke?"
"He never contacted me again."
"Pommy bastard."
"He wasn't, probably wasn't that serious about me. I don't regret it though, he was a fascinating man."
"What did he do?"
"Merchant banking but he had an interesting private life. He loved the theatre. We saw plays and opera together. It was a bit like being in the company of Byron, minus the club foot."

"Good looking?"
"No, interesting face. Very aristocratic."
"Even cultivated blokes are bastards."
"You swear too much, Frank."
"It's the mid-life crisis. Obscenities pour out of me like bile."

"That's sounds Byronic, just slightly off centre."

"Thanks." He cocked his head. "Like to head to dinner somewhere?"

She glanced at her watch. "Yeah, let's go. It too late to cook at this time of night."

"Thanks. That's a great reason to have dinner with me."

"This isn't a date, Frank."

"Absolutely not. We don't even have to sit at the same table. We could go to separate restaurants if you like."

"Don't be smart. We'll go Thai, gotta keep you lean and mean."

He growled as he stood up. "Think of me anytime you feel the need for a lean and mean man."

"This conversation's getting kinky." She lifted her bank keys out of her handbag and waited as Frank switched the lights out and set the alarm. She stared at the silver keys in the dark. They were long, slender metal. "The keys to my life," she thought. "How did my life get so small?"

Frank opened the automatic doors and they walked out onto the bohemian streetscape of Balmain. Couples sauntered around them, hands linked together or draped around waists. They wandered down Darling Road aimlessly.

Alexandra stopped in front of a restaurant. "This one's good. I had lunch here with the Area Manager last month."

"Looks busy. I'll go in and see if they've got a table."

She walked to the next shop front and stopped in front of the glass pane. At the front of the display case, pastel coloured tea lights were clustered together. Pear-shaped glass holders protected the lit candles.

"Only in Balmain," she thought, "would people leave candles unattended in a shop overnight. Bloody optimistic serendipity."

The tea lights triggered a memory. Twenty-five years ago she had stood in front of a black iron stand in St Mary's Cathedral. A ring of candles rimmed the stand's circumference and she held a tea light aloft as she attached it. Each candle represented a whispered prayer, offered in supplication to the God within.

"Look after her, Lord," she prayed. "Keep her safe."

She glanced upwards, imagined the jet crossing deep oceans and Kate asleep in her seat as she flew to a new life in England. She positioned her candle on the highest rung of the stand, then walked out of the church. She blinked hard to stem tears that rose in her eyes.

"You may break your heart but men will go on as before." She whispered, then smiled at the irony of what she said. "Now I'm quoting Marcus Aurelius. What have you done to me, Kate?"

She left the Cathedral and crossed the road to Hyde Park.

Cicadas sang their botanical hymn in the twilight. Alexandra stared at her feet, each step seemed to lead her onwards, to a dull life. She looked at the darkened sky again.

"Goodbye. You don't know how much I'll miss your war words," She thought. She slung her bag over her shoulder and made her way to the bus stop.

"Alexy, we've got a table." Alexandra started back to the present and followed behind Frank.

The tea lights gleamed in their holders.

Chapter 15

"I thought of you on Friday night." Alexandra poured Kate's tea as they sat in the back garden. "The day you left for London in the eighties, I lit a candle for you at St Mary's. I remembered last night."
"You were always a sweetie." Kate lifted her face to the morning sun. "Feel that beautiful light on your face. It's life-giving." She motioned with her hand to the garden. "I noticed something this week. I couldn't work out why the plants always look different here. You buy new ones every month, don't you? You let the old ones die, then you replace them."
"I don't mean to kill them. I sorta forget about them until they're withered stumps and then it's too late. And I don't buy new ones every month, just when friends are visiting or the oldies are coming to lunch."
"Corporate woman, let me help you! I'll water them for you while I'm here." She hesitated. "Did you notice the prints in the hall?"
"No, I got in late last night."
"Have a look, see what you think."

Alexandra ran inside the flat and stood in the hallway. It was transfigured.
On the cream walls, hung two black and white photographs, encased in thick, wood frames. Each photograph contained surreal religious iconography. A black Jesus hung on a cross. Shadows obscured his face and limbs to a blur. In the second photograph, a nun ran down the stairs of Sacre' Core, her black garment stark against a snowy landscape.
Alexandra reached up and removed the frames. She pulled out at a nail and watched as plaster puckered at the edge of the hole.
Kate was silent as she approached the table and placed the frames on the ground.
"Stop summarizing me, you don't know me that well. You haven't lived here for a long time."

She watched as Kate whitened.

"Look, I don't hate them and I'm not angry with you. It's just....."

"You're right, I apologize. If someone hung prints in my flat without asking me, I'd be livid."

Alexandra squeezed her arm. "What possessed you? You're way more savvy than that."

"Not at the moment. I seem to have lost my definition of acceptable boundaries." Kate leaned on the table and rested her head on her hand. "Have you ever lost your walking rhythm?"

"Explain, please."

"When I first arrived in London, I felt out of sync. I'd walk around the city, bewildered. The streets were crowded, I felt as though hundreds of people were lined up against me. When sometimes you're imperceptibly walking towards someone and you shift to avoid them and they shift in the same direction? You're both still headed towards each other, like silent magnets about to collide. The other person makes a showy break clear of you, and you stand still, feeling fragile." Kate stared at the garden as she continued. "Then I met Nicholas and he steered the path for me. He was older and self-assured and I followed him like a lost puppy. Now, in Sydney, I feel out of sync again."

"Kate." Alexandra held her hand. "You don't appear that way."

"I've just hammered two holes in your wall. I'm so sorry."

"Do it again and I'll shoot you." Alexandra poured another cup of tea. "How's your mother?"

"That's a part of it. She's taken over mothering Isabella, they're in sync with their cardigans, card games and manure."

"What you need is chocolate cake. Wait here."

Kate laughed as Alexandra pulled a half-eaten mud cake from her fridge.

"Staff birthday yesterday. Jenny insisted I take the leftovers home, starving spinster that I am."

"You're a tonic. It's a shame...." Kate stopped.

"What?"

"It's a shame you never married. Motherhood and marriage would've really suited you."

"I made peace with that years ago. Watching Pina's kids grow into teenagers cured me of maternal longings." Alexandra looked down as she spoke. "It was harder when I turned forty, media reports were banging on about falling fertility rates and women leaving it too late to have kids. It was like being surrounded by my own fears, made public. I grieved for what wouldn't be in my life." She whispered. "Then I was treated for depression a couple of years later."

"I didn't know! You should've told me."

"I'm lucky if I see you once every five years! I edit my words because of that. Don't tell me that you don't do the same."

"I do." Kate gave a wry grin. "Women present the front we want others to see." She hesitated. "What did you do?"

"With the depression? I saw a psychologist, took long service leave and lots of little pills."

"I'm sure Katrina was a big help."

"I never told her. Kit Kat lives in an uncomplicated reality, nothing throws her off balance. I needed her containment at that time, needed to hear her stories about the kids and the mums at school. It was my escape time. If she noticed I was different, she never said anything."

"That stoic woman."

"Aren't you the stoic?"

"That was a lifetime ago. It feels that way, at least. Nicholas hated my search for philosophies and meaning. In the end, he hated me." She looked at Alexandra. "Really, you've been the only inconstant, constant friendship in my life."

"Ditto." Alexandra checked her watch. "I've gotta go to work. Do you have plans today?"

"I'm doing whatever Bella wants today."

"Sensible. I'll see you tonight." Without a further word, she was gone, into her busy life.

Kate lifted her face to the sun again. It shone down on her, constant on its axis.

"Jane, Jane, Jane." She whispered. "Where are you?"

Chapter 16: April, 1984

Alexandra stood outside the University Auditorium in her graduation gown.

"We've never had someone with letters-behind-their-name in the family." Pina looked at the degree in Alexandra's hands. "Don't expect me to be respectful towards you."

"Of course not. The occasional tug of your forelock will do."

"Piss off."

Claudia stood behind them and listened to their banter. She smoothed her new skirt as she spoke. "Pina, don't swear at your sister."

"Yes, Ma."

Alexandra gave the paper to Claudia. "You have it."

Claudia stared at the scroll, precious as ancient papaya.

Alexandra turned back to Pina. "You coming for lunch?"

"Yeah. Ted's tagging along."

"Him again? When are you gonna find a good Italian boy? You know the Aussie boys don't cut it with the oldies."

"Tough." Pina's eyes were hard to read. "I'm not marrying some spoilt wog and playing slave for the rest of my life. Ted's fun and he doesn't expect anything from me." She glanced behind her. "Don't tell her, but we're engaged."

"No! She'll have to know eventually."

"I know, just not now. I'll tell her in a month, I'll start showing then."

They stared at each other, then laughed loudly.

"Two shocks in the space of one minute," Alexandra replied. "Trust you to steal my thunder. I may not be home when you tell her."

Pina clutched her arm. "You have'ta stand by me."

"Are you happy?"

"Yeah, Ted's thrilled, he's from a family of five. We were always going to get married, it's just accelerated our plans."

"Let's not ruin Ma's big day. This is the first thing I've done in my life that she's proud of."

"Probably the last."

They eyed each other.

"An Aunty, huh? Makes me feel old."

"You are. A spinster at twenty three and not a suitor in sight."

"Unlike you; unwed and pregnant to boyfriend of no great prospects."

"Fiancé, thank you very much."

"Show me the ring."

"Can't afford one, we're saving for a flat first. Haven't you noticed all the overtime I've been doing lately?"

"I thought you wanted to be out of the house. The oldies have been arguing a lot lately."

"You think they'd be over it by now. They're in their fifties, for God's sake."

"Do Ted's parents know?"

"Not yet, he'll speak to them the same night he speaks to ours."

"He's either incredibly brave or incredibly stupid."

"He just doesn't know how much shit will hit the fan when Ma finds out."

"I'll stick up for you."

"Thanks, Ally. What will you do with the money the oldies gave you for graduation?"

"Put it towards a deposit for a flat. With you out of the house, I'll have to get a life going."

"You gonna move out?"

"No, I'll rent it out for a couple of years first. Ma will be easier to live with if there's a grandchild she can adore nearby."

Pina murmured. "Not so close, we're going to live in the inner city somewhere. Ted wants to be close to the architectural practice, he hates travelling. Anywhere past Glebe is the 'burbs for him."

"Might inspire Ma to get her license. Of course, it depends what said grandchild is like." Alexandra nudged her. "I can't believe you're going to be a mum. Over protective and obsessive, I presume?"

"Hopefully, I'll be laid back. Maybe some of Ted's sanity will rub off onto me."

"If it does, pass some on."

"I will. So, letters-behind-your name, are you going to take a holiday and visit the rellos in Italy before you land a job?"

"No, I'm gonna work for a couple of years, then travel."

"The sensible approach. Ma will be proud."

Alexandra was silent as she watched Pina wave at a figure approaching in the distance. The man started to run towards them and Pina's smile widened. She beamed at him as he reached them. Ted wove around the crowd and hugged Alexandra.

"Congratulations, big white hope."

"Thank you, soon-to-be-mud in my mother's eyes."

He looked behind and saw a radiant Claudia standing with Emilio. "That's what Pina keeps saying. At this rate, I might shoot through."

Pina spoke. "If you do that, I'll kill you." She motioned to the crowd. "Ally, is Nick here?"

"No, he graduates on a different day."

"He's a nice bloke. And he didn't get as blotto as the rest of the guys at your 21st."

"He's a cool guy. We'll stay in touch." Alexandra turned away. "We can't stand here all day, basking in my glory. Let's go eat." She approached Claudia. "Ma, Ted and Pina are hungry. Especially Pina."

Pina's eyes widened.

Claudia stared at them. "Okay, let's go." Degree in one hand, beloved child in the other, she walked down the stairs.

Alexandra turned back to grin at Pina and Ted. They walked hand in hand and the sunlight caught Pina's eyes as she smiled at Ted. He rubbed her stomach protectively and Alexandra's heart caught within her chest. She turned away and walked onwards with her mother.

Chapter 17

"I've got a job."

Alexandra stared at Kate as she dried the dishes. "Where?"

"A call centre in Newtown, four days a week. Bella and Mother are absolutely furious with me, as will be Nicholas when he finds out."

Alexandra made no comment.

"I've also got a short term lease on a flat in Annandale. Three months starting next week."

"You've made some decisions then."

"I wish. I'm trying to provoke Nicholas to make a decision. We never resolve an issue, things fester for years. It's always been that way. You don't approve, I can tell."

"I feel for Bella."

"I know. She'll start school here in a different grade and curriculum. She misses Nicholas and her friends, so it's a lot stacked against her." Kate spoke in a low voice. "But it buys me time."

"Couldn't you send her back early? You don't intend to stay in Australia forever, do you?"

Kate leaned against the kitchen bench and stared out the window. A hedge of native flowering shrubs separated the Art Deco apartment building from the next block. Wattlebirds suckled flowers from the hedge.

"I don't know. I've missed this landscape. It's like something has seeped into me again and I want to see where it leads." She lowered her head. "I bought some charcoal pencils at Glebe markets the other day. Wait here."

Alexandra watched her re-emerge from her bedroom, sketchpad in hand.

"What do you think?"

Alexandra caught her breath. It was a sketch of herself reading in the back garden. "When did you do this?"

"Yesterday afternoon, from the lounge room. You were carried away by an article you were reading, the light caught your profile well and I couldn't resist. Hope you don't mind." Kate hesitated. "It's the first sketch I've done since I left Australia. I felt like my hand was on fire, my veins alive..." She looked away. "I never felt like that in London. But here, I feel bold again." She laughed. "I sound mad, don't I?"

"No, I've felt like that once. In London."
"You mean, with him?"
"Yes. I never had that carefree time in my twenties, like you did. I always felt like I had the weight of my mother's dreams on my shoulders. I used to imagine you, walking through Christopher Wren's London, hair swinging free, the way your hair does." Alexandra spoke softly. "I was here in Ashfield, accumulating assets and barren memories." Her throat tightened but she continued on. "In London, I lived my twenties in six intense weeks. I wasn't my mother's sensible daughter, I was another girl. He didn't know about my life and I didn't want him to. Then I came back to Sydney and that girl went away and she never came back. Whenever I feel sad or regretful, I think of him." She stopped abruptly. "I think we need a cup of tea."
"No, you sit outside and I'll bring it to you." Kate handed her the pad. "You can critique my sketch."

Alexandra walked outside. She stared at the sunburnt grass, at the fence and tried to focus. It was no good; memories of London filled her senses. She stared at the pad and glanced inadvertently toward the sketch of her younger self. A black haired girl in a sunlight bush, alight with youth and dreams. She looked down and traced the new sketch with her fingertips. A middle-aged woman reflected back at her, with her mother's Roman features. Lines fanned out from her eyes, joined a deep laugh line creased into her cheek. She sat on a chair, hair swept back in a clip, shoulders bent in relaxation. The romantic writers of her youth long banished to dusty bookshelves, her older self read a magazine recipe for banana bread.

She placed the sketch down and watched Kate approach the table with a tray.

"Well?" Kate motioned to the sketch.

"You captured me too well, there's nowhere to hide from that."

"You don't see it like I do."

"I see my years very well."

"But not your loveliness, you were always blind to that."

"I see my mother's nose and a middle aged woman blobbing out for the afternoon."

Kate hugged the sketch close to her chest and didn't reply.

"I do see your skill. You were born to be an artist. The talent I saw twenty five years ago is still there, just dormant."

"Thank you," Kate spoke softly, "and the heart I saw twenty five years ago is still there. Just dormant."

"Touché."

They sat in silence. The sun was positioned directly above them. It lit the landscape in blazing clarity. Not a shadow could be seen.

1977

The blanket was prickly. The fibres tickled her nose and Alexandra sneezed.

"Yuck. Cover your mouth, you pig! I've got your germs all over me."

"Shut up, Pin! It came out before I knew it." Alexandra pulled at the blanket and wrapped it around her flannelette pyjamas.

"It's freezing, Ally. C'mon, share the blanket, will you."

"No." They tussled on the sofa. Pina stood and wrestled the blanket from her grasp.

Alexandra spoke. "Since you're up, close the door."

"I'm older than you, it's my duty to boss you around. You do it."

"No, Bill Collins is just finishing his introduction to the movie. I wanna listen."

"Well, we won't hear it anyway. They're at it again."

They both looked up from the sofa, to the hallway beyond. Shouts reverberated through their parents' bedroom door.

"Putana! You never paid for anything. I give you my wages every week, what more do you want?"

"I work for you and the girls. I want to see my village one more time."

"They don't want us there, they never did. You are a crazy woman, like your family."

"You make me that way."

A cupboard door slammed and both girls started.

Pina spoke softly. "Don't cry. You'll just feel worse." She walked across the room and slammed the rumpus room door shut and turned the volume up on the TV. She crept back to the sofa and snuggled close to Alexandra in sisterly intimacy.

They listened to the witty banter of the 1930's American film classic. The black and white screen blurred with interference and a buzzing noise sounded. The image cleared and Spencer Tracey smiled down at Katherine Hepburn. Pina's hand pulled at threads on the cushion, till shreds hung in grotesque bunches. Another door slammed in the distance and she murmured. "They'll go on forever. I don't know why Dad doesn't try to make her happy."

"You mean like Fred and Ginger? Or Spencer and Kate? I don't think our oldies could talk like that. They'd have to like each other first. And they don't."

"No." Pina pointed to the screen. "Look at Spencer Tracey, I can't believe he became famous! He's so damn ugly."

"But Kate Hepburn loves him. I wonder if they liked each other in real life. Y'know, if they got married."

"Ally, don't you know anything? They had an affair for years and he was already married to someone else. If you ever got your nose out of a book, you'd learn something about the world."

"Like you, you mean? Who's having sex with who, that's a lot of important world news to know."

Pina threw a cushion at her. "Shut up, I'm trying to listen to Spencer."

"First names, huh? You shut up, I'm listening to Kate."

They leaned back on the sofa, trying to concentrate. The shouts in the background persisted.

Alexandra frowned. "You'd think they'd be embarrassed that the neighbours can hear them. I hate going outside to hang the washing when they're fighting."

"Must be their Italian blood. Maybe that's the way everyone speaks to each other in Italy."

"I'm never getting married."

"I'm marrying a cool Australian guy," Pina whispered back. "No bloody wogs for me."

"You have'ta find someone who wants to marry you first." Alexandra replied. "Maybe Dad could offer a dowry for you; a years' worth of vegetables from his garden. Maybe throw in one of the chickens too."

"Very funny. He'd have to sell the whole house to get someone interested in you."

Alexandra clubbed her with a cushion and Pina flung one back. They tumbled to the floor below, pelting each other with frayed cushions. A sharp thump sounded near the TV.

"Shit, you hit the T.V. screen! You've knocked the antenna off."

"I didn't, you bloody did it! Pick it up, Dad'll crack if he sees it."

The image went fuzzy as they crouched close to the screen. Pina held the antenna aloft and Alexandra examined the effect.

"No, further over to the left, bit more to the right. That's it! Stand there for the rest of the movie."

"Very funny, Ally! I wish Dad would buy a colour TV. We're the only kids in high school that don't have one." Pina placed the antenna gingerly on the TV top and sat back down to view the result.

"He'll just go on about the depression and the war if we ask for anything new. We'll have to steal one."

Pina replied. "Can you imagine how much shit would hit the fan if we did that? Mum would beat us to a pulp."

The door jerked open and Emilio's stared down at them. "What was that noise?"

"I can't tell you, Dad, but it was all Pina's fault."

"Rubbish, you did it!"

"Enough, your mama and I can't sleep. Pina, you are nothing but trouble, always. Now, silenzio." He slammed the door and the girls stared at each other.

"Nice talking to you too, Dad." Pina muttered. "He calls that trying to sleep? Who's he kidding?"

"Forget it," Alexandra leaned her head on Pina's shoulder. "We've already missed the beginning of the film. I think Kate told Spencer off for something stupid he did."

"Bet she didn't make him cry."

They lapsed into silence.

Alexandra wrapped her arm around Pina as the shouting began again in the bedroom. A fragile peace surrounded them as they watched the flickering images on the television. Pina pulled at the cushion and Alexandra exclaimed.

"You're wrecking it! Here, give it to me." She placed the cushion on her lap and patted it. "Go on, lie on it. Just don't fall asleep and start snoring."

Chapter 18

"I'm thinking of writing to him." Alexandra lay on the grass in Balmain Park.

"You mean the English prick who dumped you?" Frank sat alongside her, long legs stretched out.

"Yes, him."

"What for? It's obvious he doesn't want to know you."

"I don't know why he's never contacted me and neither do you. He could have a perfectly good reason."

"Alexy, I thought you were street smart."

She sat up. "Have you finished eating lunch? We should head back to the branch."

He pulled a blue flower from the grass and waved it under her nose. "He loves you, he loves you not."

She pushed it away. "Piss off, Frank."

"Professor Freud to you. Did you know Freud used this treatment on his patients?" He pulled the first petal from the flower. "He loves you." He lay the petal on the grass and pretended to adjust invisible glasses on his nose. "Now we all know that if ... Miss Cossetto, what is your ex's name?"

"Edward."

"Precisely. Now if Eddy loved you.."

"Edward!"

"That's what I said. If Eddy loved you, he would have declared his devotion at the end of the holiday and begged you to stay. Did he?"

She shook her head.

"I see." He pulled the next petal. "He loves you not. If he didn't love you, he would have shaken your hand at the airport and thanked you for being a good roll in the hay. Did he?"

"No, of course not!"

"Aha, Professor Freud finds the situation is not as clear cut as he first thought. Further psychoanalysis is needed to discern the emotional state of steady Eddy." He tugged at another petal. "He loves you." Frank looked directly into her eyes as he spoke. "If he loved you, he would have hounded you with funny letters and cards and called you all manner of endearing names pertaining to your homeland. For example, Kanga, as adopted by Prince Charles. Or Bilby, Walla or my little possum. Did he?"

"No."

"I don't know why not. You're a fine example of Australian womanhood and as worthy of a ridiculous handle as the next woman."

"Thank you, Professor."

"You're welcome. Professor Freud recognizes the need to flatter his patients into baring their innermost souls. I do it well, don't I? Subtle yet probing."

She nudged him. "You're up to he loves you not."

"Please, you can't rush genius." Frank tugged at the next petal absentmindedly. "He loves you not. If he didn't love you, he would have presented a facade the whole time you were together. This manner of role-playing is self-protective. The innermost thoughts and desires are not truly shared. Did he do this?"

Alexandra spoke. "I don't think so."

"Let's see. Did he tell you embarrassing things about himself?"

"Like what?"

"That he's an obsessive tooth flosser?"

"No."

"That he farts at the slightest movement he makes?"

"God, I only knew him six weeks. You don't tell that to someone you've just met."

"I do."

"And you're still single. I rest my case."

Frank nodded. "This grey area of flower therapy remains unresolved. Next petal." He placed it on Alexandra's lap. "He loves you. The minute you were gone, he rang travel agents and checked his annual leave, planning his first holiday to the colony."

She held the petal in her hand and spoke softly. "I don't know the answer to that one."

"But Professor Freud does. Have you seen him in Sydney in the last ten years?"

"Not recently."

"Aha, once again Professor Freud succeeds in his flower therapy. You may shred the remaining petals at leisure. Free of charge."

She lifted the torn flower from the grass. "What were you up to?"

"He loves you."

She continued counting. "He loves me not, he loves me, he loves me not." She stared at the remaining two petals silently.

"Like me to finish it?"

She shook her head. A bird sang and she looked up at the carefree trill. Alexandra pulled the last petals simultaneously and dropped them to the grass. "He loves me."

"You cheated."

"I was never good at maths." She checked her watch and stood up. "C'mon, we're late. I've gotta organize the girls' rosters for the next month. How's the dating service going?"

"No need to smirk, Alexy. Heaps of people do online dating. You should try it." He motioned to the torn flower on the grass. "But you're waiting for Lord Byron to contact you via snail mail."

"You're a rude bastard."

"Don't hang onto a dream. The gospel according to Doris Day won't get you far nowadays."

She was silent as they walked back to work.

Chapter 19: London 1995

She was still young. Alexandra peered at her face in the compact mirror as she applied her lipstick. No matter how she tilted the glass, her face appeared unlined in the late sun.

Nicholas glanced at her from the driver's mirror. "Australian ritual?"

"No, universal female ritual. I was checking for wrinkles."

Kate looked back from the front seat. "You look the same as when we last saw you in Sydney. Have a child and then see wrinkles spring up." She tickled the feet of the child seated beside Alexandra. "Here's my wrinkle-maker. Keep mummy up at night, won't sleep in of a morning, wrinkle-maker."

Isabella giggled and drew her foot away.

Alexandra whispered to her. "You can stay with me in Australia, if Mummy needs some wrinkle- making free time."

"Yes please. Do you have a kangaroo in your house?"

"No, but we can visit them at the zoo." She tapped Kate's shoulder. "What are you teaching your child about Australia?"

"Same lies as everyone else. Kangaroos and koalas on every street corner."

Isabella had picked up her colouring book and Alexandra bent down to her. "Draw me a princess, please. I'll hang the picture in my flat at home."

Isabella held the pencil with an unsteady hand. "I'll draw a prince too. A princess needs a prince, everyone knows that."

"Of course."

"Do you like boys?"

"Yes."

"Do you have a boyfriend?"

"No."

Kate turned to Isabella. "Should we help Alexandra find a boyfriend? An English prince?"

Alexandra replied. "I think William and Harry are a bit young for me. An Earl or a Viscount would be nice. Not too old, must be able to breathe independently."

Nicholas interjected. "We don't move in such salubrious circles. I do know a few merchant bankers and lawyers. Would they do?"

Alexandra turned to Isabella. "What do you think?"

"No, only a prince."

"They're a bit thin on the ground, Bella. I'll buy my own tiara and consider the merchant banker option".

Isabella stared at her. "What?"

Kate tapped her daughter's foot. "Pardon, not what."

"I don't know what she said."

"Alexandra, not she."

Nicholas glanced across at Kate. "Steady on, she can't banter like an adult."

"I'm not correcting her understanding, just her grammar."

"I think she does pretty well. She doesn't butcher her vowels the way you do."

Kate was silent.

Alexandra stared out the car window. The countryside of Surrey reminded her of the colours of a child's paint box. Rich, primary colours; a contrast to the subtle hues of the Australian landscape.

The silence in the car continued.

Isabella sketched her crayon princess. The stick figure wore a lopsided tiara and a wide smile. A giant sun shone above the princess, the yellow rays spread over the page.

"We'll head back to Kensington, the weather's turning."

Kate remained silent at Nicholas' words. He stopped at a set of lights.

"War words," thought Alexandra, "they exist here too".

Her hand played with the door handle as she watched commuters enter a train station entrance on her left. She half-opened her door. "Do you mind if I catch the train back to Kensington?"

"We've scared you off." Nicholas spoke.

"Not at all," Alexandra leaned forward. "I haven't caught a train in England, just buses around London. I'd love to explore a bit on my own. I'll be back this evening. You don't mind, do you, Kate?"

"Go, enjoy. Get off at Parliament and explore the Thames."

Nicholas pulled over. "She can go where she wants."

Kate turned away.

"I can't wait to see my princess picture," Alexandra smiled at Isabella. "Don't forget to colour it in for me." She closed the car door before the little girl replied and she watched as the car pulled away from the curb. Isabella stared at her through the darkened glass.

Cool air on her skin. Alexandra looked at the village bustle about her and thought of her own suburb. Ashfield was a mix of many races. Vietnamese, Lebanese and Chinese entrepreneurs ran businesses as old Mediterraneans sat in cafes, sipping espressos.

"People walk slower here," she thought, "perhaps it's indicative of a long settled race". She watched as people weaved around her. "What happened to me?" she wondered. "Thirty four years old and travelling overseas for the first time. What took me so long?" She caught her reflection in a shop front mirror and stared at it. "An unlined face of a life little lived." She thought. "I had no courage." Alexandra turned away and hurried to the train station. She purchased her ticket and descended the stairs to the crowded platform.

"Mind the gap please." The automated voice on the loud speaker warned passengers of danger.

"Cautionary advice to a cautious woman," she thought.

Terraced suburbia passed before her eyes as the train sped on. "I'm unsettled here," she thought "my quiet pattern of living is disturbed". She remembered Isabella's eyes as she left them and the strained silence beforehand. "They're starting to hate each other." She mused.

Drops of rain splashed against the train windows, their shape distorted. She stared at the unknown suburbs that sped past.

"Mind the gap please." The voice heralded the train's arrival at Kensington.

London felt cleaner, its smog dissipated by the rain. Alexandra wandered past terrace shop fronts, filled with expensive antiques and fashion. She examined leather bound books, arranged on a high bookshelf, the names impossible to discern. The cracked spines indicated classic English literature and she longed to pull one down and delve into the pages. As she walked on, she heard voices ahead and saw camera lights flash in the dark. A section of road was cordoned off and a crowd of people stood at barriers, held back by police guard.

"Diana!"

A sleek limousine pulled up against the curb. The camera flashes intensified as a tall, beautifully proportioned blonde woman emerged from within. The crowd called to her as she strode ahead to an art gallery entrance. "Diana!"

Alexandra stopped, caught by the spectacle. She brushed her jeans down, to remove traces of crayon and gathered her cardigan closer. She stood at the back of the barricade. The princess entered an art gallery, painted minimalist white inside. Vibrant, modern art hung on the walls.

"She's there!" A woman pointed to her left and all heads turned.

The princess' face was partially obscured, as she stood surrounded by an elegant throng of patrons.

Alexandra glimpsed her famous smile as she bent to speak to an elderly woman, who held a glass of champagne in her frail hand. Diana's aristocratic features were thrown in sharp relief and a thrilled murmur went through the crowd.

"Poor girl," muttered a woman beside Alexandra. "Her life's like a play, played out to an audience."

Alexandra replied. "We're born in the same year. I've always been fascinated by her."

"You're an Aussie girl," the woman smiled. "My son's there now, for his gap year."

An elbow jabbed into Alexandra's side and she winced and moved away. Her departure went unnoticed as she crossed the road and continued on her way. Tears sprang from her eyes and coursed down her face. The street scene of Kensington blurred around her as she stopped at a lamp post and covered her face. Her tears were unstoppable and she bent closer to the post.

"God, what's wrong with me?" she thought. "What am I crying for?"

Chapter 20

Kate started at the brisk knock at the door.

Isabella looked up as Kate bent to straighten a cushion. "Don't bother. Grandma will hate the flat anyway."

Kate walked to the front door.

"Here I am." Rosemary stood at the doorway, her handbag tucked into her arm. She opened her arms wide and Isabella ran to give her a hug. Kate watched them in silence.

"Cost me an arm and a leg to get here." Rosemary looked at Kate. "Cab drivers charge a small ransom to ferry passengers about."

"You didn't drive?"

"I have a restricted license." Rosemary turned to Isabella. "Don't grow old, dear. Invisible chains begin to fetter you at seventy and they don't stop." She walked inside the flat and stared at the lounge room. "It's hard to believe you can accumulate clutter in such a short time already."

Kate stared at her stooped frame and how the years had bent her spine. "Take your cardigan?"

"Please. What are you working on, Isabella?" Rosemary walked across to the dining table and lifted a book from the pile stacked on the table.

"Australian history."

"Are you finding it hard, dear?"

"No, I've just got to catch up. I don't know as much as the others in my class."

"And your other subjects, Maths and English. How are you in those?"

"Ahead, especially in Maths."

"It's a shame your mother has pulled you out of a good British education."

"Not now." Kate motioned with her hand. "Come sit on the sofa."

Rosemary pulled out a dining chair. "No thank you, I like a firm chair." She watched Isabella as she bent over her textbook. "It will be harder for her to catch up when you return home." She stared about the room. "Why you don't see something through, Kate, I'll never know. I offered you stability and security when your father died. I didn't run away."

Kate bowed her head as she replied softly. "I think I've done a good job with Isabella. You've said yourself that she's a lovely girl."
"In spite of your topsy-turvy parenting."
"Enough."
"Mum, don't start. Grandma's just arrived."
"Your grandma started the minute she walked in the door. Didn't you notice? All her empathy towards you, implying that I was the reason for everything that's wrong in your life." Kate continued. "I invite you for lunch and you can't wait to start criticizing me. It's a habit with you. Do you ever wonder what started me on my meandering life? Did you ever link it to your parenting?" She caught sight of Isabella's eyes but continued on. "You diminished me, every comment pigeon-holed me as something negative. I wasn't a dreamy child to you, the way Dad saw me. I was unreliable. I wasn't imaginative, to you I was flighty."
Rosemary replied. "According to you, I've done it all wrong. All children feel that way about their parents. I'm sure Isabella will say something like that to you one day. The only difference with you is that you've gone on blaming me for your life, whereas you are responsible for your own poor decisions."

"Poor decisions come from poor building blocks. You never supported me, like Dad did. All I saw of myself was what I saw through your eyes. For you, that was a daughter who didn't live up to your expectations."
"Poor you, eh? Growing up with a mother like me."
"Cut the irony. You've never been able to speak to me without demeaning me." She glanced at her daughter. "Sorry, Bella. Grandma and I can't spend an hour together without arguing. I'll get lunch ready and you two can talk."

Rosemary replied. "You're right, we always squabble. Not nice for you to hear, Isabella."

She motioned to the lounge walls. "Did the owners leave the artwork behind?"

"Mum and I bought them at flea markets at Glebe and Newtown. Cool, aren't they?"

"I never understood modern art. Always found it alarming. I prefer the master painters who knew how to draw. Most modern artists throw paint at a canvas and pretend it means something." She stood and walked across to a canvas. "This is lovely. See the tilt of the woman's head? This is a proper picture."

Isabella looked across. "I like it too. Mum sketched it."

Rosemary turned to Kate. "You're drawing again? Is this part of the teenage rebellion you're going through at the moment?"

Kate stood at the kitchen bench as she replied. "Yes, I'm sketching again. That's Alexandra, can you tell?"

"No! I didn't see it that clearly. It is too! My word, she's aged. She looks just like Claudia. It's been so long since I've seen her parents." She nodded. "You don't show your years as much."

"That's what Alexandra said." Kate stared at the sketch. "I think she looks beautiful."

"You'll never sell anything if you sketch a subject too accurately. People like to be flattered." Rosemary peered closer. "Far too many wrinkles in that profile. She can't look that old surely?"

"No, twice as lovely."

Rosemary had stopped in front of another sketch. "This is Isabella. But you haven't finished it, Kate."

"I have."

"No, the lines on the face are incomplete. You can't see her expression clearly."

"I did that deliberately. She's a teenager, there are no hard lines to her yet, her face is as fresh as an impressionists painting. I wanted to sketch the promise of her life to come."

Rosemary replied. "With that philosophy, you'll never sell a thing, I guarantee. It's a shame because you still have skill. If you take after me, you'll be crippled with arthritis in ten years time and will have lost your chance to establish yourself. Be practical, Kate. There's a market out there for traditional portraiture. Great artists are discovered young, the rest plod along like we all do. Make the best of what gifts you have, don't waste more time." She moved away from the wall. "You were never a make-do child, were you?"

Kate opened the fridge door with a jerk and pulled meat from a shelf. She slammed the door.

Isabella looked up. "Mum."

"It's OK. Grandma's free to criticize." She stared at the slab of meat.

"Pepper and salt, dear." Rosemary called out. "It needs pepper and salt. And a pan, it won't cook by itself. Do you want me to help you?"

"No, thanks."

Sunlight warmed the small kitchen. Kate squinted in the glare. A tree branch ran parallel to the window and a stem of leaves pressed against the glass. A leaf was flattened against the pane, its fine veins exposed in the light.

Kate thought how easy it would be to crush the delicate leaf. She just needed to clasp it in one hand.

Chapter 21

"Frank called for you." Claudia looked at her daughter. "Is he nice?"

"Why did he call here?"

"He wanted to tell you he couldn't bush walk this weekend."

"Could've left a message on my phone."

"I think he wanted to talk to you." Claudia winced as she leaned back on her chair in the back patio "We had a nice talk, he's a polite man. No swearing, like men today do."

Alexandra remained silent.

"Is he nice?"

"Where's this leading?"

"What, leading? I'm just asking my daughter a question." Claudia looked at a cluster of flowers in a garden bed as she spoke. "Not nice to be on your own when you are old. My mama was fifty five when Papa died. Everybody leave her alone in the village, and me, I can do nothing for her in this country."

"I'm not lonely. I see Pina and the kids all the time and I have my friends."

"It's not the same," Claudia murmured. "Your papa and I, we are together fifty years. I don't know why God didn't make anyone special enough for you. But he has his ways, no?" She turned to Alexandra. "My daughter's heart is wasted on a bank." She stared at the hunched figure of Emilio, as he pushed a wheelbarrow across the back garden. The expression in her eyes was unreadable.

Alexandra stood. "I'm gonna talk to Dad."

"Watch the thorns, Darly. Too many thorns this year."

She walked across the garden and stopped at a neatly trimmed hedge. Emilio had crouched over, spreading a charcoal substance over the soil. He picked up his secateurs. "I give you some flowers to take home. Remember to put them in a vase and add some sugar."

"I will."

"Anything growing in your garden, Alexandra?"

"You know there isn't. What are you doing?"

"That's the first time you ask me anything for the garden. Not like Pina, she was always beside me, ask me questions about this flower or this vegetable. You hide in the house with your books and stories. Too much time dreaming. That's why Pina has a husband and children and you have career and walking. Things that don't need worry for."

She waved her hands. "Enough lectures for one day. Have these roses always been here?"

"See what I say? You have no eyes for the small world, just the big one. I planted these roses the first year your mama and I moved here. You cut your finger chasing a ball over there. Claudia, she was angry with me, said I didn't care for my daughters as long as I had my roses. She was too much worry for you girls." He lifted the head of a rose. "Smell, Alexandra. Such perfume you can't buy." He glanced up. "The sun is too strong, it will burn my vegetables."

"You say that every year." She bent down to the soil and racked the embers with her hand. "What's this?"

"Wood ash from the barbeque."

"I didn't know you used that for compost."

Emilio lifted an eyebrow.

"Don't say it, Pop."

He handed her a bouquet of orange and pink roses. "In my country, we say that something must die for something new to grow. Ashes for a new life."

She accepted the flowers and headed back to the patio. The roses started to close inwards, in sync with evening tide. Alexandra held the roses loosely in her hand.

Chapter 22:   London, 2000

"Edward's dropping by tonight."

Alexandra stared at Kate.

"The merchant banker friend of Nicholas. You met him briefly the last time you were here."

"The very quiet man?"

"He's not really. He'd just separated from his fiancé at that time and had taken a battering. He's the nicest of Nicholas' friends, doesn't patronize me." She stared out the window at the drizzling rain. "I miss blue skies. Makes you feel braver."

"Why do you need to feel brave? You moved to a new country and started a new life. I stayed in Sydney, got a job in a bank and I live ten kilometres from my parents. Blue skies didn't do much for me."

Kate remained silent and Alexandra squeezed her arm. "Are you homesick?"

"I don't know if I'd call it that. Because my parents were English, it seemed my destiny to come here." She continued. "I just wonder what I'd be like if I stayed there.... Come; let's pick up Isabella. She hates waiting at the school gates. It's a nice walk, most days."

Alexandra followed behind her as they left the apartment and walked down to the street.

"This is a novelty for me. Sydney's so dry at the moment. They say we're falling into another drought."

"A sunburnt country, a land of sweeping plains." Kate murmured as she walked along. "It's seems impossibly far away. I should take Bella home to see Mother again, she barely remembers her. I just hate staying in that house." A cab swept past them and drenched their lower legs with a spray of rainwater.

Kate linked arms with Alexandra. "Maybe I could, after all. Do you see Katrina much?"

"We catch up. She's busy with the kids but I go over for birthdays and Christmas drinks. Kit Kat's good at networking."

Kate looked ahead. "Is she happy with her life?"

"You still ask the big ticket questions. Katrina lives in a calm bubble, chaos theory doesn't figure in her life. Her glass is always half-full."

"Lucky her," Kate murmured. "Look, Alexandra. How lovely." She pointed ahead.

A London bus drove past with its headlights on. The beam illuminated pools of water collecting on the pavement. Trees appear to droop in the downpour, their leaves sodden with rain.

Kate spoke. "I love the quality of light in London. It has a nebulous feel, it blurs the edges of the streetscape. When Bella was in her pram, I'd walk for miles around Kensington on rainy days. I couldn't understand why other mums didn't venture out into Hyde Park with their babies. It was like walking in a dream, all the hard edges of life removed. You couldn't tell if it was early morning or dusk." Kate held her hand out to catch a raindrop. "Remember the day at Falconbridge at Lindsay's house?"

"God, we were so young. Do you know that's Katrina's favourite memory of Uni?"

"No! I always felt she didn't approve of me, that she found me flighty."

"She did."

They glanced at each other under their umbrellas.

"Katrina's too pragmatic for your artistic nature. She's a straight shooter."

"She made me feel insecure, I felt excluded from her common sense. You could sit on the fence and not betray yourself. If I tried to do that, I would have gone insane." Kate continued. "Nothing ever works out the way you expect. I'm sure you've noticed that Nicholas and I aren't getting on spectacularly well. Even on your first visit it must have been obvious." She hesitated. "When I first met him, he seemed like a god: an older man in control of his life. I was flattered he loved me. He organized me and I let him, to have the order I craved in my life. But we just grew tired of each other's needs. They were like welts that never healed."

The rain created a teeming veil for Kate's words. "I want an unstructured and spontaneous life. If you met the school mums, you'd understand why. They have a gene I wasn't born with, a brittle love of conformity. When I'm near them, I feel I'm choking."
She motioned ahead to the iron school gates that enclosed a series of red brick buildings. "See the women standing on the left hand side? They stand in the same position every day and talk about work, gym, their perfect houses and children. We're very polite to each other and say the right nothings but I feel like an observer. Like something's missing inside me because I can't find meaning in that life." She murmured. "Existence is suffering, and the path of suffering has a cause."
"Mr Aurelius?"
"No, Buddhist philosophy."
Alexandra squeezed her arm. "All marriages go through low points. I remember you and Nicholas when you first visited Sydney, so full of promise. Hang on, Kate. I'm sure it will improve if you give it time."
"I do, for Isabella's sake. I know what it's like to grow up without a father. She adores Nicholas and he's a great dad. Maybe I want too much, I cry for something that doesn't exist." She straightened her shoulders as they approached the gates. She leaned close to Alexandra. "The school committee crowd. They hate me because I only help out on creative art day-one day a year! They practically live at the school, with canteen and fund raising. I hate their bland lives."

A tall brunette called out. "Kate, I've been waiting for you. If I don't invite Isabella for a visit this week, my Jessica will kill me."
"We can't have that, can we?" Kate pulled Alexandra close to her. "Meet my dear friend, Alexandra. We've known each other since University days."
Alexandra watched as Kate spoke her lines perfectly.

Chapter 23

"He's almost ugly." Alexandra thought. She twirled her glass of champagne between her fingers as she listened to the conversation.

"It doesn't look anything like Delia's recipe." Kate set the pudding on the table. "I've cocked it up. This is only going to taste decent if I drown it in cream. Apologies in advance to your arteries, Edward."

The quiet man tilted his head to one side. His features caught the chandelier light and Alexandra stared at him. He had a weary persona, even his clothes looked careworn. Edward wore his greying hair in a short, military cut. His face was long, with angular features that suited middle age. Lines fanned vertically from his eyes to a wide, thin mouth. He moved and the chandelier threw his forehead into shadow.

"Perhaps Nick could open a decent bottle of red, in compensation for your culinary disaster. If we could rouse him from his drunken stupor on the sofa."

Nicholas cocked an eye open. "I'm not that selfless, Edward. Neither are you for that matter."

"I know, but I don't have children. How do you manage?"

"Kate's selfless enough for both of us."

"He's not kidding." Kate poured cream on Edward's serve. "What do you think?"

He bent forward. "How did you manage to bake a dessert that has no aroma at all? That takes a rare talent."

Kate refilled her champagne glass. "Bloody Delia Smith! I followed her recipe to the letter. I swear she doctors them."

"Perhaps there's some convict blood in you, that wants to poison your guests."

"You're half-Australian, Edward. You understand me."

Alexandra spoke up. "How are you half-Australian?"

"My father impregnated an Aussie girl during a brief sojourn in the sixties. Then he moved us back to the sunless homeland ten years later. My mother never settled in England and she returned to Australia when I started University. I stayed with my father." He bent his head and the shadows fell across his cheek and into his eyes. "So I have a decade of Aussie in me. Enough to create a shield against English neuroses."

Nicholas called out. "Careful, Edward. We only invite you to dinner to make up numbers. And Kate feels sorry for you because no-one likes you."

"Nicholas," Kate looked at him. "Everyone likes Edward."

"No, they don't. He comes here because you collect strays."

"Women adore him."

"Only for brief periods of time. I've known him since university days. It's the same pattern: he meets a girl, she loves him passionately for a brief period of grace, then loathes him for eternity."

"What a thing to say in front of your guests!"

Nicholas remained silent.

Alexandra spoke. "You speak about him as if he's not here."

"Thank you." Edward looked at her and another shadow fell on his face and obscured his lips. "Too much time wasted on me. I preferred it when we were laughing at Kate's pudding. Which by the way is sublimely awful. More cream, please."

"Of course." Kate absentmindedly emptied the jug over the remains of his dessert and he grinned at Alexandra.

"Now you know a bit about dysfunctional me, albeit by third parties."

"I don't believe any of it."

"Believe it, I'm the product of the migrant experience in reverse, uprooted from the new country to the homeland. Kate tells me that you, on the other hand, are the classic migrant tale."

Kate stood and walked over to where Nicholas lay. She sat on a corner of the sofa and draped her legs across him. He lay, impassive to her touch as she tickled his chest with her foot. He pushed her away and she moved across to the kitchen, nursing her drink.

"She always gets a certain look on her face when she speaks about you," Edward whispered. "I had to talk to you at least once, to find out why."

Alexandra shook her head. "Obviously something deeply disturbed about me too."

"Obviously. What is it?"

"I won't go into it. I like to appear as normal as possible, especially to strangers."

"The very people you should be yourself with. Never know when a kindred spirit is lurking nearby."

"Kindred spirits are rare, nearly extinct. All my friends in Sydney are married, with kids. They invite me over to give me what they think I don't have."

"Exactly. What do they have anyway? And do we want it?"

"No." Her eyes followed the shadow that fell onto his cheek as he turned towards her. "Perhaps you live a life in the shadows too." She thought.

"What are you thinking?"

"Pardon?"

"You're thinking. Can't hide it, I'm afraid. You have a very expressive face."

She looked away.

"Even your silence is expressive."

"What are you saying, Edward?" Kate sat on the kitchen bench, her champagne glass clenched between her legs. "Alexandra looks aflutter." Her blond hair hung limp on her shoulders and she drained her glass quickly. "Keep her that way," she murmured. "It's good for her."

Nicholas cocked an eye open. "Are you stirring up trouble?"

"Always."

Edward bent towards Alexandra. "It's your turn to be spoken of in the third person."

"I don't like it. I've always been a control freak, I'm afraid." She lifted her glass. "Might as well finish it, I'm drunk anyway."

"Champagne should be sipped, not sculled."

"Depends on the company."

He glanced across the room. "I'll drink to that." and emptied his flute. He poured the remains of the bottle into their glasses and Alexandra shook her head. "I'll have an awful headache tomorrow."

"Best cure for that is a moonlight walk. Shall we?"

"Yes."

Edward held out his arm and she stood.

"That was fabulous, hostess with the mostest. You can poison me anytime."

Kate held out her arms and hugged Edward. "You can come anytime."

"Wish I could."

"Now you're being drunk and dirty." She stared at him from her perch. "Take Alexandra with you."

"I am." He tapped Nicholas on the arm, who rolled away on the sofa, snoring.

Kate watched them leave, her glass clenched in her hand.

Chapter 24

An insignificant rain fell, unacknowledged by either of them. She felt her life had blurred. The only clear sensation she felt was Edward's grip on her arm. A breeze ruffled unseen leaves in the dark. A cab halted on the street and revellers spilt onto the pavement.

"It's never quiet here," she murmured. "Ashfield shuts down at midnight."

"You live at Ashfield? I lived at Haberfield as a child."

"The better side of Liverpool Road."

"Not according to my father. Nothing about Australia was better than England. Not even the climate and beaches."

"How did he reason that?"

"He said the heat made Australian women look like prunes at thirty."

"Did you miss Sydney when you left?"

"God, yes." His grip tightened and Alexandra moved away slightly. He eased his hold on her.

She motioned to the street. "Kensington reminds me of the 1920's; velvet gloves, hansom cabs and gaslight."

"I'd never thought about it like that before. Locals are stupid about their own town."

"True."

"Nothing like Aussie honesty. Are you always so blunt?"

"Too much."

"Do tell."

She shook her head. "I'm too drunk to be discreet. Don't want to regret anything in the morning."

"You won't remember."

She stumbled as they turned a corner and Edward held onto her. "Oops a daisy."

"Now you sound like Noel Coward."

A memory of the boy in the nightclub flashed into her mind, the scent of masculinity close again. Her eyes wandered the length of Edward's shoulder, examined the close-cropped hair and thick neck.

He motioned to the streetscape. "I nearly went mad when we first arrived here. Our street in Haberfield didn't have paving and guttering, so it had a bush feel to it. Our neighbour had gum trees in his front garden and kookaburras would nest in them. They called out every morning and I thought it was the most beautiful sound in the world. My father wanted to kill them, said he couldn't sleep when they started chorusing. He joked that sleep deprivation made him return to England."

The rain added intimacy to their meandering pace as he spoke on. "It was dirty and crowded in Kensington. I woke early with the traffic sounds and wait for the kookaburra call. I didn't know it was native to Australia. When I found out, I cried for weeks. My father told me not to be so stupid."

The breeze picked up and Edward held her closer. "Before we left Australia, we went on a country holiday, just outside of Canberra. We camped on the banks of the Murrumbidgee River. I couldn't believe the bird life I saw; flocks of black cockatoos and galahs. Brilliant flashes of colour that lit up the sky. I felt like I'd fallen into heaven, I was barefoot and dirty the whole trip." He continued. "Except when we had a day trip into Canberra for my father's business. His suit got crumpled in the car and he was furious that Mother couldn't press it. He liked to control us and it drove him mad when he couldn't. My mother was totally different, she was open to life in ways my father couldn't be."

"You didn't want to go back home with her?"

"No, I'd just applied for a position at University and wanted to earn a million dollars and emigrate as a rich businessman. That didn't work out either."

Her heart caught as she listened. "Do you stay in touch with your mum?"

"Phone calls. She never came back to London. She felt like an imposter the whole time she lived here. Like her blood was imprinted with a different stamp and she couldn't re-stamp it. Kate reminds me of her sometimes."

She nodded.

He bent his head closer to her and his grey hair gleamed in the street lamps. "I ran away the day before we left Sydney. I caught the train to the city and ran to the Botanical Gardens and sat in a tree and cried for hours."

"You poor little kid." She squeezed his arm. "Obviously you made it home in time for your flight."

"Yes, I didn't fancy the life of a street urchin. Self-preservation kicked in at an early age. Before I left the garden, I carved my name in the tree, so my city wouldn't forget me."

"Where in the garden?"

"In a bottle tree. Somewhere near a bay alongside Lady Macquarie's chair."

"Must be Farm Cove. I'll have to see if it's still there."

"Thank you."

The rain increased and she shivered. Edward drew her closer still and the sensation resonated within her.

"You build a life where you are. I made a brilliant crowd of friends at University. Then I bought a small flat at Kensington when I started work. My father encouraged me to be clever with my money and I have to thank him for that advice. I could never afford to buy into Kensington if I was starting out now." He stared ahead. "Kids are resilient. They survive catastrophe or at least what feels like it. It would have been easier if I had siblings, we would have bonded together. Only children see the world through adult eyes and if that vision is jaded, we adapt likewise. I have the cynical vision of my father embedded in me."

"Do you see him much?"

"Rarely. I call him on his birthday and he calls me on mine. He talks business and I respond with polite words. His second wife is nice. Pricks always marry well. They marry women that reflect the humanity they lack."

"Is he that awful?"

"No, he's that normal. Most men marry to get emotional connection. Vivian is very surface driven, she has a neat garden and a beautiful home. She's a member of her local bridge club. She doesn't have time to notice my father has no heart." He stopped and smiled at her in the dark. "I'm telling you everything about myself. You have eyes that lure people to speak about themselves. Where did you get eyes like that?"

She kissed him on the lips and he pulled her close. "Come back with me. My flat's close by."

She nodded.

"I warn you, it's a one bedroom flat. Not enough room to swing a dingo."

"Why don't you sell it for something bigger?"

"I love it too much. I walk everywhere; to work, the theatre, to friends. It clears my head. I could sell up and buy a place in the suburbs but my heart doesn't belong there. Too many families on the loose and small, noisy dogs."

"I love to walk, too. I'm part of a bush walking group."

"Where do you go?"

"Within a three hour radius of Sydney. Mostly the Blue Mountains and the Royal National Park. They're a brilliant crowd of people. They saved my mind a few times over the years."

"Why have you needed saving?"

"Early mid-life crisis. I was always an advanced child."

"And the migrant experience for you?"

"Similar to yours. My parents, particularly my mum, loved us not wisely but too well."

"The reverberations were Shakespearean?"

"Yes but I was luckier than you, I had an older sister. Pina fulfilled all their expectations: good husband, two children. All I offer them is my career."

"Never came close to marriage?"

"I never wanted too. My mum was so needy. I needed distance from that, I wanted to create a different world for myself, meet someone knowing I didn't have to rely on them financially. My mind-set was trained to protect myself from any hint of neediness. I didn't ever want to be dependent, like she was with me." She caught her breath. "You seem to have luring eyes as well."

He led her to the side entrance of an early 20th century red brick building. The iron railing on the staircase bannister felt slippery under her hand.

Edward opened the door to his flat and motioned with his hand for her to enter.

She stood shivering in the room, as Edward switched on a lamp.

She stared at the empty room. "You're not big on possessions, are you?"

"I don't like encumbrances."

"I didn't realize a sofa was an encumbrance." Alexandra stared about her. She stood in a small lounge room. It was bare except for a corner lamp, an old TV and large cushions, strewn across the floor. The walls were painted deep terracotta, offset by a white washed, ornate ceiling. Posters of Covent Garden operas and Drury Lane productions covered the wall space and she examined them. "How gorgeous, they suits the room so well." she spoke softly.

He stood behind her and nuzzled her neck softly. "My ex fiancé didn't think so. We actually broke up because I wouldn't take them down. She insisted I have them framed professionally, if I had to keep them. She said I was too old to have posters on my walls, like some overgrown schoolboy. In her eyes, I needed furniture and a career trajectory to be whole. In the end, she said I was too immature for her." He shrugged. "I'm glad I said no."

"I don't know why people do that to each other. Fall in love because of something endearing about the other person and then try to change it down the track. I couldn't imagine giving up my old furniture and books for someone else."

He walked across to the cushions and pulled her down. He held her close and kissed her on the lips. "Do you ever do things on a whim?"
"As a rule, no. But drunk and on holidays, apparently, yes."
He whispered. "I could love a girl like you." He leaned on his elbow and traced the line of her breasts with a soft hand. "I can't offer you anything."
"I'm not asking."
He was silent and awkward then and she made it easier for him. Alexandra took off her wet cardigan. "What you have and what you offer me is enough."

He held the small of her back and caressed her hips. The blurred, wet night outside seemed to permeate her body. A series of yearnings filled her as she felt his strong hands. She felt blood rise to her face and was glad the flat was unlit and unfurnished. The empty space resonated with her, like a post modern song and she alone understood the melody. "It's more than enough," she thought.

Covent Garden

She looked about the crowded theatre. "It's raucous," she whispered to Edward.

"The show hasn't started yet, so we're allowed to misbehave." He leaned close to her and his hair brushed against her cheek. "My mum took me to pantos when we first arrived in London. That's when I realized I could survive my new life. I swamped my love of the bush for the crude fun of theatre. Grease paint for gum leaves. It comforted me."

He kissed her hand. "I loved it so much, I decided I wanted to be an actor. Mum enrolled me in kid's theatre and I felt I could be anything. I still remember the drama teacher's deep voice and the damp smell of the studio. However, my father disapproved and he stopped my classes after a year." His eyes were unreadable in the dim light and Alexandra squeezed his hand. He held her hand tightly as his arm rested on her lap. Alexandra stared at the nonchalant gesture.

She looked at her program and examined the list of actors. "I started to attend the theatre when I finished Uni," she spoke in a low voice. "I hadn't ever been to a play before. My parents were in survival mode in Australia. They didn't have the knowledge or money to explore the cultural side of life. The first production I saw was 'Waiting For Godot' and I'll never forget the sensation of discovery. It was as if I was living in a different country, one of thought and beauty and intellect. I didn't know it existed before then and I had no intention of letting it go, ever."

"I couldn't live without it, either."

She squeezed his hand and glanced about the theatre. It was richly painted with velvet-draped stalls. Elegant Londoners in satin and silk buzzed around the seats, accepted her silently as a member of their city. She held Edward's hand and waited for the curtain to rise.

Chapter 25

"We've both shunned opportunities."

Alexandra looked across at Edward. "Pardon?"

He changed gears and the car revved forward smoothly. "I miss driving. I'd move to the country tomorrow for the sheer pleasure of driving on expressways."

"What car would you drive?"

"A 1970, olive green E-Type jaguar." He glanced across at her. "I know that sounds pretentious but a friend of Dad's had one when I was a child and I thought it was glorious."

"I guess it's not practical to park it in a one bedder in Kensington."

"No."

"What did you mean before about shunning opportunities? Like careers?"

"Partly. You're happy in middle management, not ambitious to get a more powerful position. I'm the same, I've got men fifteen years younger than me as my superiors and I don't care. I never wanted to be too successful, it felt like wearing shoes that didn't fit. I couldn't say the right, corporate, suck up words to get ahead. I couldn't stand the idea of having the perfect wife and 2.2 kids in the suburbs, either. So I evaded every career opportunity and sabotaged every relationship I ever had because I couldn't pretend to want that life. I think in a different way, you've done it too."

"No, I shunned everything because I was afraid." She stopped and looked out the car window. They drove along a hedged lane. Cottages lay hidden by the dense foliage, countless lives lived in the quaint stone and thatched abodes they passed. Flower baskets hung from narrow ledges, with a profusion of spring flowers. She spoke again. "My mama told me stories of her life when I was a little girl. I was enthralled by them, especially her stories about her cousin. They were always sad and I absorbed her melancholic view of life, almost by osmosis. I felt I was party to her secrets and only I could make her happy and protect her when she was grieving. But it was too great a burden for a child and when I was a teenager, I needed to be free of her sorrow. I would live my life surrounded by things I could control and I'd never be touched by grief or neediness." She continued. "Of course, the opposite happened. The opportunities I threw away came back to bite me."

"Did you ever meet your mum's cousin?"

"I don't know what happened to him. I stopped listening to her stories. I was the typical, ethnic teenager. I loathed my background and my parents. Pina was worse though, she gave them hell till she got married."

"There's always one wild sibling."

"So you've known Nicholas since Uni?"

"We were in the same economics class. He was a Public School boy, always very focused on career and always successful with women. Kate was a surprise, she seemed so soft and young, compared to the girlfriends he'd had before. He jumped at the chance to play Svengali and she seemed content. It seems to be unravelling somewhat, now."

She was silent as they turned into a quiet lane. Oak trees lined the road and the enormous trunks cast thick shade, creating a dappled, sunlit road.

"I want to have a ploughman's lunch."

He lifted an eyebrow.

"I hear about them all the time on British TV shows. I want to try one."

"As you wish. I'll warn you now, I'll fight you for the cheese platter."

"Savoury or sweet palate?"

"Savoury."

"Last meal on earth: chocolate ice cream or pickled gherkins?"

"Gherkins."

"No wonder we get on so well. Our stomachs are kindred spirits too."

He tugged her hair. "I'm serious about the cheese. Especially if it's blue vein."

Alexandra nodded and wound down her window. Unknown bird song sounded from the countryside and she absorbed the strange calls. She glanced at her watch and the date gave her a pang. Three weeks of her holiday had passed already. She shook the thought out of her mind as Edward spoke again.

"If it's Brie or a French Camembert, I'll share a small portion."

"Ditto."

"We're five miles from my dad's place. That's his local golf course over there."

"Do you want to drop by and say hello?"

"God, no. I've never introduced anyone in my life to him. Never will."

"Good approach to life. Men seem to have that black and white view down pat."

"Are you insulting me?"

"No, just pigeon holing. It's a female past-time."

He accelerated to a higher gear. "Miss Cautious, two can play that game. Fearful child, were we? Let me play on that fear." He sped down the narrow road and she pulled at his arm.

"Slow down, Edward, it's working."

He eased up on the gears and she nodded at him. "You got me."

"I hope so." He muttered.

She looked across at him and started. A section of road was exposed to the sunlight and the light caught his profile in relief. She saw a glimpse of him as a young man, hair blown back in a youthful tangle and his features relaxed. Instinctively, she moved closer to the window and looked away.

Chapter 26

"Walk with me."

Edward rolled over to Alexandra's side of the bed. "Now?"

"I need to. Please."

"It's 6.30 on a Saturday morning." His long limbs a lazy tangle under the sheets.

"I'll meet you in the hallway." She dressed quickly and waited at the front window. Street lamps were extinguished and light struggled to illuminate the city dawn. She stared at the portion of overcast sky she could see from the window.

"It's fresh out there. Take this." Edward held out an outsize cardigan.

They left the flat in silence and headed in the direction of Hyde Park. Edward tried to hold her hand. "It's like holding hands with a soldier," he murmured. "You don't walk, you stride along. Have you always marched like that?"

"Yes. I was taught by Irish Catholic nuns at Primary school. They played British military music at assembly and we marched to our classrooms. We boiled in the sun but we never missed a beat. They were tough old birds."

"Sounds kinky."

"No, they were bullies in wimples. It's funny isn't it, you need to be away from your country to remember it clearly. I can almost hear the marching music."

"We're not far from Buck Palace. Perhaps Lilibet's rousing the troops."

She slowed down and linked arms with him. "It's been five weeks. Has Kate said anything?"

"No, she's told Nicholas not to ask any questions either. He's been remarkably restrained." She shook his arm off. "It's no good, I can't stroll. What do you like to do?"

He raised an eyebrow at her.

"When you're home on weekends. You know, down time stuff. Apart from the theatre and seeing friends."

He was silent awhile. "Not everyone's as active as you. I have a small life, I probably don't go further than ten kilometres from London all year. Except when I holiday. Then I must go somewhere sunny, with blond, white-toothed waitresses and crowds of people. Then I don't notice I'm alone."

"Poor you. Why don't you holiday with friends?"

"Do you?"

"No."

They reached the gates of Hyde Park and Edward struck a path. Alexandra pointed to a large sectioned area underneath an oak tree. The grass was left uncut and long shoots grew wild.

"I love those grass patches. We could never do that in our public parks in Australia. Every snake for ten kilometres would congregate in it."

Edward stared at the field. "My dad liked capturing funnel web spiders when we lived at Haberfield. He dug them out of the front rockery and poked a stick at them till they hunched up, ready to attack. He just laughed, the mad man. I didn't have that adventurous gene. I'd stand back, trembling, while he lifted the jar for me to hold. Once he pretended to drop it over me, the prick."

"What did you do?"

"What any six year old would do, burst into tears and run away."

"Has he mellowed in age?"

"Now he's an octogenarian prick. Decades of consistency in my family."

She linked arms with him.

"I thought you couldn't do stroll."

"Being Australian, I'm extremely flexible."

"I've seen that in bed."

She laughed. "I leave in another week."

"I know." he stopped abruptly and pulled her onto the grass. Their lips met in a kiss. "Live with me."

"In Kensington?"

"No, Hyde Park." He ruffled her hair. "I love a girl who doesn't mind if I do that, some women can't bare to be ruffled."

"You need to buy some furniture if I live with you."

"I could commit to a sofa. Or we could watch TV in bed."

"That's way too Americanized for my taste."

"You're right, we'll keep the bedroom for sex alone." He growled in her ear. "I can't let you go. Stay."

"I don't know," she whispered. "What would I do here?"

"Kept woman, chatelaine, muse, earth mother. That would keep you busy for a while."

"I'd need a job, otherwise I'd feel pointless. And I couldn't live in London penniless."

"Why not? The rest of us do."

A cuckoo sounded in the trees and she glanced upwards. A ring of trees shielded the call as it echoed in the thicket.

"My mama loves the cuckoo," she murmured. "It was her favourite bird song as a child."

"It's an omen then."

"It's a fluke."

He bent his head and walked in silence. She felt the pressure of his hand as they walked along, each finger distinct against her palm. "I'd love to." The words remained unsaid, caught in her throat as she imagined the life she could have. Walks in an ancient city, a bare flat warmed by culture and kindred thoughts.

"I don't know, Edward."

"You suit me."

"I bet you say that to every insecure woman you sleep with."

"I don't."

She thrilled at the words, felt their truth.

He pulled her close, slipped an arm around her waist. "I'm not offering marriage." He tilted her face close. "It doesn't make sense to me. It's like listening to a crowd singing at a football match, the same senseless ode their father sang, without thought or intent. I never understood that mentality. But you're kin to me, as otherworldly as my own heart feels. I don't think you want the traditional deal either. Please say yes."

In the damp dawn, held by this extraordinary man, Alexandra thought back to the day at Falconbridge. The warm grass beneath her, the sun on her limbs as she listened to war words.

"Kate was right," she thought. "Love words need risk."

She let go of him and motioned to the path. "Walk with me."

Chapter 27

"Cheer up, Edward, at least you're not eating my cooking." Kate leaned across the restaurant table and squeezed his hand.

He stirred his coffee. "Small mercies." He rubbed Alexandra's thigh as he spoke. "It's more like a wake than a dinner. We need champagne."

Alexandra watched as he signalled a waiter. She memorized the motion, as she had other small moments of the last six weeks.

They sat in a French restaurant, comprising the narrow frontage of a Kensington terrace. Small tables created a circus-like trail for waiters to navigate. Cream table lamps gave the dining room a period elegance. The wallpaper fascinated Alexandra. An Art Deco patina of black velvet swirls across a creamy background. Photographs of early 20th Century Parisian life hung in nooks. Alexandra stared at the swirls as Edward spoke, his voice seemed to attach to the refined pattern. She wondered if this background would replace his face in her memories. Resonant tones caught within black velvet.

Kate spoke. "I knew you would like each other."

Edward replied. "A bit more than that."

"Excellent," Kate raised her glass for Nicholas to refill it. "So what's next for you Continent-crossed lovers?"

"A holiday," Edward leaned back in his chair. "I'd like to see Australia again. See what it feels like to be back."

"If it feels like home." Kate whispered.

Nicholas saw the expression in her eyes. "No-where is home for you, orphan. You yearn for the past, like a child with a burst balloon."

She turned to Edward. "You will, of course, be an obnoxious English tourist, the sun will be too hot, the people too brash. You'll beg Alexandra to come back with you and she'll say....." She turned to Alexandra, who continued to stare at the wall as she replied.

"That's too fast for me. We'll just take it as it comes."

Kate leaned closer to her. "Is he not the story book hero of your dreams? All I need to do is knock out an eye and cut off half a limb and he's complete. Crippled but complete."

Nicholas held her arm. "Go slow on the wine tonight. You're already talking about dismembering our host."

Kate shook him off. "Alexandra understands me. Don't you, Jane?"

Alexandra shifted in her seat. The black velvet loomed threateningly close. "I don't see Edward like that. You should know me better."

"I'm not so sure. You've waited a long time for your hero."

"I think you should stop now."

"I'm just curious."

Alexandra spoke quietly. "We'll see what happens."

"You mean, see what pans out? See the lay of the land? What the universe divines? Is your life to be summarized in clichés? Isn't Edward worth more than a cliché?"

"Kate!" Alexandra bent her head as she spoke. "Please."

"We'll walk back tonight." Edward broke in. "We don't need a lift."

Nicholas replied. "It's raining, you don't want to send Alexandra home sick. What will her family think?"

Alexandra interrupted. "I have an umbrella."

"She does," Kate spoke in a low voice. "Alexandra has precautions for all unforeseen events. Even her indiscreet moments are bound in time frames. You'll become a time frame too, Edward."

Alexandra shook her head. "I don't know why you're saying this. Playing prophet again. Just like you did at Uni."

Kate looked away.

"She does it at home." Nicholas broke the silence. "No occasion too special to be ruined by Kate's rantings." He leaned away from the table. "Isabella thinks an hysterical mother is standard parenting."

"I'm not hysterical." Kate drained her glass. "You can't discern emotional clarity, that's all."

"Is that what this is? I thought it was sour grapes, that you can't stand to see someone else happy."

"You don't know me very well, Nicholas."

"After fifteen years together, I know you well enough."

Kate was silent.

Light conversation floated around them amidst the chink of silver cutlery and crystal wine glasses. "Great choice." Alexandra spoke to Edward. "I've only been to one French restaurant in Sydney. Mostly I like Thai in Newtown or cheap eats around Marrickville."

"Wait till you try my favourite haunts in Paris. This pales in comparison."

Nicholas interjected. "This is serious, if Edward is thinking of taking you on a culinary tour of his beloved France. Very few women are offered a chance to travel with the great man." He looked at Edward. "Do you remember how poor we were at Uni? Every week, you insisted on buying a good Brie and a loaf of French bread, to supplement the stodge we ate the rest of the week." He leaned towards Alexandra. "Girls found his Francophile traits very attractive. Cheese was an inspired way to their hearts."

"This girl can eat me under the table." Edward rejoined. "You should see what she can do to a cheese platter."

Alexandra shrugged her shoulders. "European upbringing."

A waiter squeezed past their table and Alexandra watched his graceful contortions as he served entrees to a nearby table. Four plates were stacked on his arms as he bent in the dim light to take a wine order. "It's a skill." She murmured. "Like a live cabaret and we're the players."

"That's what I love about France," Edward leaned close to her. "Theatre at every turn. You must come with me."

She nodded as she sipped her coffee.

Kate had sat back in her chair, nursing a glass of red.

Nicholas nodded to her. "We should give them some time together on their last night. I know Edward is taking you to Heathrow tomorrow, so I'll say goodbye now, Alexandra." He bent and brushed her cheek. "Hope you enjoyed the trip."

"I did, I loved it."

Kate stood, her blond fringe half-concealing her eyes. "Make it special," she said loudly. "Be brave with each other." She walked away and Nicholas followed her.

And they were gone. Alexandra sat in silence.

"She can be bloody annoying."

Alexandra replied. "And embarrassing."

"Was she like that at Uni?"

"Mysterious and difficult? Always, that's what I love about her." She paused for a moment. "I hope you don't think that I regard you as some kind of...." Her voice trailed off.

"No, I don't." Edward closed the bill wallet. "We both know what we wants. Let's go."

She was silent as they left the restaurant. The air was cold as they stepped outside.

Edward linked hands with her and she ran her free hand over iron balustrades as they walked along.

"You look eight years old when you do that."

"Thanks, that's my travel age when I'm abroad." She stared at the sandstone terraces and curved street. "I'll always associate you with Kensington."

"That sounds like a farewell."

"No, it's a statement of fact. You're a part of this area, as much as the shops and terraces."

"I've never been likened to a shop before. Dysfunctional bastard, yes."

A young couple approached them, they faces turned towards each other in fury.

"You've done that for years to embarrass me and I hate it." The young woman lowered her voice as she spoke. "I'm sick of it."

The man kept his hands thrust into his jeans pockets as he walked on with an annoyed countenance. Edward waited until they passed, then pulled Alexandra to a stop. He looked up at the sky.

"Is it full moon? I always fought with girlfriends more at that time of the month."

Alexandra shrugged. They walked on, side-by-side, no longer touching.

"It's a truth universally acknowledged," Edward spoke softly, "that romance shrinks in accordance with the number of years one is married. I'm amazed that no one's ever formulated the mathematical equation. What area of maths do you think it involves?"

"Percentages?"

"Perhaps it was Einstein's last, great, unfinished formula."

"Perhaps. Or the principle to be learnt is don't marry."

"You're a quick pupil."

She was silent and he nudged her. "Penny for your thoughts."

"None to be had. I was thinking that I start work on Tuesday and my desk will be stacked with sales targets and reports."

"Too prosaic."

"Life can be prosaic."

He was quiet as they reached the apartment. He held her arm as they entered the glassed front door of the block. She slipped her shoes off as she stood in the bare lounge. The fireplace remained unlit, as it had since Edward bought the apartment. The chill of the flat seemed sharper tonight. The Covent Garden posters appeared ghostly in the dark, as she wandered the room.

The bedroom light clicked on. Off. She walked in quietly and saw his thickset outline in the moonlight. Images imprinted, stored beside velvet swirls. She slipped into bed beside him and Edward reached out to her. He stroked her back. "I can't tonight. Middle aged man's curse, too much red wine."

"I'm happy to cuddle." He curled towards her and she held him close. She watched shadows fall on inanimate objects. A shadow fell over Edward's face and she waited for it to pass away.

I'm not good at speaking about myself, never have been really. Only ever did it once in my life.

I came here because I had to.

Personally, I've always believed you have to be strong and work out emotional problems yourself. That's what I've always done. But I need a psychologist to sign a certificate so I can get sick leave from my job.

Whom did I confide in? A man I knew briefly. He was lovely. He understood me instinctively, it was like we had a sub-text from the start and didn't need to play twenty questions. But that was a long time ago and it didn't work out. I made peace with it.

No, I don't want to say his name. That's private.

I'm depressed and I need time off work. May I have the certificate?

I don't know when it started, I was still in Primary school. Every afternoon when I walked home from school, I'd pass the rock. It stood in front of a fibro house, built after the Second World War for ex-service men. The streets were full of those houses in the sixties, like suburban army messes. It was a stark landscape, all the native trees were removed from the blocks of land. It was like the council believed the veterans didn't deserve to have beauty in their lives. The lines of their life had to be as in wartime, desolate and ugly.

Somehow, this rock was left to stand when the housing commission houses were built. All the kids from school would climb it on the way home. The boys would pretend it was a rearing stallion and play cowboys and Indians on it.

I was suspicious of it, didn't like the way it stood out in the landscape. It looked jarring and dangerous. That's when I started the routine. I had to circle the rock three times before I could walk home the rest of the way. It was like the rock controlled me, somehow.

I knew it was silly but I couldn't stop. Even if I managed to walk home without circling it, I'd go back. I knew it made it all right, if I circled the rock. I was free of obligation then.

I don't know why I did that. Kids are weird, aren't they?

We didn't laugh much as a family. My parents worked really hard to build a new life here.

It's easier for the second generation, Australia's home to them. Pina's kids have a clear idea of their homeland. There's no past traditions placed before them on an altar of memories and longing. We never knew which country was home; the old or the new one?

I remember the first time it happened. I was walking home from netball and my coach walked part of the way with me. It was so hot, my ponytail clung to my neck.

My coach was really nice, her name was Susan. She asked me questions about my life, what I liked to do, who I played with at school.

I had no words to say to her, I was sweating in fear. I felt sorry for her, wasting her time on me. I had no words about my life. How could I? I was nothing at all.

When do the words come back? In crowds. In large groups of people, I exist.

If people try to tee up a social date, I only go out in a group. It feels safer. If they want to talk one on one, it's unsettling.

There's nothing to talk about if it's just me, I exist only in crowds. It doesn't work any other way.

There was Nick, an Australian boy, studying engineering at Uni. He was so cute, girls would stare when I spoke to him.

He always wanted to go for coffee, to talk to me alone. But I made sure we were always in a group. That way he wouldn't know I had no words of myself.

Anxious? Am I? I always feel this way, I don't know how else to be. Isn't it ok to feel this way? Tired of what? No, I've got to be in control of it all. Otherwise, there's nothing left.

Men? I'm not made for love. Some people don't do intimacy. I was bone tired before I was twenty, I had too many secrets to carry as a child.

Sometimes Mama would go away and Pina and I never knew when she was coming back. She would stay in hospital for up to a week to rest her nerves. I felt I'd failed her. A good daughter would have protected her, right?

I knew when I was a little girl, that she didn't love him. I didn't feel shocked or sad, I just knew.

It was like we had a secret and I was special enough for her to share it.

Of course, when I became a teenager, I hated her sadness. She never smiled for me.

Keepers of secrets are always reserved for tears, aren't they?

When Edward held me in his flat in Kensington, I felt the loss of my youth. I'd never been brave or clever enough to change my life, unlike Kate.

He's a sweet man. I loved everything about him, his effusive words and his lack of possessions. He felt like home to me. And I know he loved me, enjoyed my honesty and acceptance of his life.

I could only be brave for a little while, for the length of the holiday. Edward asked me to live with him, but I couldn't do that. My mama would never understand that kind of life, she believed in tradition and the values of marriage. He would be alien to her, a bohemian leading me on the road to ruin.

I only told Pina about him. That way I could keep him to myself and I could pledge my heart to a dream. It helped me sleep at night, though.

At the airport, I made it clear that we were over. And all without words. He tried to talk about the future and us but I was cool towards him.

At the departure lounge, he tried to hug me and whisper something in my ear. I just stood back and shook my head. In my mind, I'd already said goodbye. I just wanted to store him in my memories, it was too frightening to make it real. I couldn't even say goodbye.

But I paid for it, endlessly.

It's like I had a double life. Whenever I spoke to or touched someone, I wanted to know who he was speaking to, who he was touching.

Like an ever-present shadow in my life, a void I could never fill by motion or thought.

I had to let go of him, or the senselessness of it would have driven me mad. The void lapped at me, if I was bush walking or out to dinner with friends. I wondered where he was, who was by his side.

I'm part of a bush walking group, we meet every weekend. I joined it soon after I moved into my flat. Once I started walking, I finally realized what homeland I belonged to.

Frank? Do I mention him a lot? I didn't know. He's a good mate, a funny bastard. Can laugh at himself, not many people can.

Frank's like me, we don't have a regular life. We press our faces against invisible windows and watch other normal lives. We're comrades in arms that way. I couldn't see him in a romantic way.

I'm glad I'm not young anymore, it's easier to be invisible now.

My life is like a set of parallel lines. If I keep to a straight line and don't veer off course, then everything's OK. If I veer slightly, then chaos happens. I live a parallel life to Edward, along a path that drives me to futility. But I accept it quietly. I learnt it was best to creep around softly as a child, or too much anger and sadness would follow me. If I were quiet and stayed between the lines, it would be all right.

That's when it started. They call it the black dog, don't they? It's more like a black wolf, it grips your heart with fangs.

I wanted to die some days.

It's like when you watch T.V. You see the most outrageously cruel things happening, in places like Africa: children with matchstick legs and swollen bellies and you don't feel anything. Desensitized to the point of indifference.

Depression feels like that. I don't feel anything, just blank. The other day, I went out for coffee with the girls from work. They were teasing me, trying to lift the sadness from my eyes. I laughed at the right times, pulled the right faces. But inside, I was blank. If they tried to touch me, I would have withered away.

Now I was completely nothing, inside and out.

I sleep a lot. Sometimes, I'm so tired, I lay on the couch all day. Then I get up at four in the morning, have a hot bath and lie down again. It's weird because I've always been a busy girl, always on the go.

Pina brings me dinner two nights a week. We never talk about the depression but I see the worry in her eyes. She blames him and I let her.

I'm such a coward.

I'm the product of an anxious mother. I remember walking to the shops with her as a child; I had to walk to the right of her, so a car wouldn't hit me first if it veered off the road.

The sexual revolution of the sixties must have frightened her, a bewildering contrast to her village life. No wonder she hid us away.

I remember in primary school, I once tried to sketch a scene I liked. It was a picture of tundra grass, waving in the wind. I could see it clearly in my mind's eye but I didn't have the skill to translate it onto paper. I burst into tears and Sister Imelda tried to comfort me. It should have been a fun activity but I was a nervous wreck because of my failings. Like there was an invisible bar I was always trying to reach but I wasn't good enough. Anxiety feels like that.

I'm forty-three years old now. I'll never have kids or a normal life now. Like Frank, I'll watch from the sidelines. No, I don't hate my mama. She did the best she could with what she had. She never walked out either, that counts for a lot. All those years, she was so unhappy with my dad but she stayed.

I'm not shaped to hate anyone. Life's a lottery ticket, you don't know how to live when you're young. I guess even the pointless bits have purpose.

Did I tell you it's lifting? Yesterday, I sat outside with my withered plants and I heard a kookaburra call on the fence. It tilted its face to the sun and began to sing.

For ages, I couldn't hear that call. It triggered memories of London and my transplanted English boy. I think subconsciously, the call was an echo to my lying heart, of all the false dreams I created about him.

But when I heard it yesterday, I didn't cry.

Chapter 28

"Have you written to him?"

Alexandra jolted out of her reverie. "Who?"

"Lord Byron."

"No."

Frank turned to Beth. "Such an expansive answer. Do you agree?"

The older woman tucked her red, layered hair behind her ears. "I'm a bit bewildered by this conversation. I thought Byron died a couple of hundred years ago."

"I'm talking about Alexy's English boyfriend."

Beth looked at Alexandra. "What Englishman?"

"It happened a long time ago, I never mentioned it."

"Was that when you came back from London the last trip?"

"Yes."

"And you were really quiet for months."

"No, I wasn't."

"We were concerned about you, even Roger noticed you were different." Beth stopped short in her tracks. "That was when my Teddy died. You were so good to me, listened to all my stories about him. And you had your own stories to tell....." She shook her head. "I'm so much older than you, I guess you talked to your girlfriends instead."

Alexandra didn't reply.

"I'm going to walk ahead, too much of a dawdling pace with you two." Beth increased her tempo and strode into the bush track.

Bird song resonated in the tree line above them. Soft pawed thumps sounded metres away, as ferns brushed against them in the dense bush.

"Frank," Alexandra spoke. "You've hurt Beth's feelings. I never spoke about that time in my life."

"No," He stared at her. "I just asked a question."

"Bullshit! You know I don't talk about my life to everyone."

"To anyone, you mean. You compartmentalize your life so minutely, I'm lucky you talk to me."

"I don't tell you everything."

"I know."

"Frank, I didn't mean that. Sorry."

He was silent and Alexandra looked at the serene sky.

"I should have talked to Beth, I know, but I wasn't brave enough to make it real. She would have offered practical advice and continuously asked me if I'd contacted him."

"But you loved him."

"Yes."

"Alexy, what's wrong with you? If I loved someone that much, I'd walk over glass to see them again." He walked ahead of her and Alexandra struggled to keep up.

"Make way, Beth. Steam roller coming through."

She stood aside for Frank. "How's the dating service going?"

"Do you want the truth, or my usual jolly lies?"

"Up to you."

"It's crap. I'm over social politeness, I'm sick of wearing my best clothes and listing my good traits over dinner. I just want to be with someone that likes me, not ticks me off a checklist of desirable traits. It's enough to turn a bloke gay."

"Gay men would hate your dress sense. My son came out years ago and he lectures me on my clothes. I make more effort for him than I do for my daughter! You'll meet someone, Frank."

"No, I was born thirty years too late. I belong in the era when women looked for a good, unremarkable provider. I've missed my chance. I hate the dating scene."

"I'd date you, Darling, but I'm too old for you."

"Thanks."

Alexandra was silent as she listened to them.

They stopped at a railing and looked at the gully below. Beth pointed to a bush at the base. "Look at that banksia! There's been a fire through here only last summer. The bush can regenerate so quickly from a pile of ash."

Alexandra thought of her father's words. "Ashes for a new life." She was silent as Frank and Beth walked ahead of her.

"Frank!" she called softly but he was too far ahead to hear her.

Chapter 29

Kate walked in the dark alongside Alexandra. "Are you sure Katrina wanted me to come tonight?"

"Yes, she invited you." Alexandra opened the front gate. "Smell the jasmine, it's growing over the fence. Too divine."

Tea lights were scattered on the brick pathway. Alexandra slipped on a mossy patch and Kate caught her.

"It's dangerous in the suburbs. No wonder I don't venture out of the inner city much."

"I've never been to a Tupperware party." Alexandra spoke. "Pina once dragged me to a Nutrimetics party, run by a cheerful blonde. She took one look at me and sold me half the catalogue. Traded on my insecurities, the cow. I spent $150 that night and I've never used the stuff since. No, I lie, I did use the face mask as weed killer once. Worked a treat, too."

Kate squeezed her arm. "I'll clutch onto you for Dutch courage. Large gatherings of suburban women frighten me."

"You didn't ever do this in London?"

"It didn't do the rounds of my set in Kensington." She smiled as Alexandra pressed the buzzer. "Best foot forward. Hopefully not in mouth."

Laughter sounded from the corridor as Katrina opened the door. "Hey, you two! Welcome. So glad you could make it." She ushered them inside. "Everyone's hitting the champagne, so I don't know if anyone will be conscious during the presentation. I should take credit card imprints now. It's a shame really, I'd love the bonus present for higher sales."

"We all desire our thirty pieces of drachma." Kate murmured as she walked down the hallway.

Katrina followed behind. She walked over to a tiny, expensively dressed blonde woman. "Suzan, you've met Alexandra before. This is Kate, we've known each other since Uni days."

"You're the one from England, with the only child." Suzan smiled. "I worked in London for two years before I married my husband, Tony. Amazing to think I had a life before my three kids took it away." She turned to Alexandra. "Are you still single?"

She nodded back as Suzan continued on. "Gosh, what's that like? Out to restaurants when you feel like it, without the juggle of kids and responsibilities. Must be bliss."

Kate's eyes narrowed. "I don't think you'd be the type to forget anything."

Katrina stood back as the two women spoke.

Suzan turned to Kate. "How's your daughter liking Sydney? Must be culture shock, coming from London."

"Isabella's desperate to fit in. She's trying to flatten her vowels but she sounds like the Queen attempting slang. We both do."

"I sounded like that when I came back. Don't worry, the Aussie strine will come back to you. Katrina tells me you're staying indefinitely."

"Isn't everything in life indefinite?"

Suzan took a sip of her champagne. "Is Isabella enrolled at a good school? We've got the girls at Santa at Strathfield, with the nuns. Locked away behind high fences till they're eighteen. Tony says he'll let them out on Saturday afternoons when they finish school."

Katrina spoke. "I think they'll make a break before then."

Alexandra nudged Kate as she spoke. "Perhaps we should head to the dining room, I think the presentation's ready."

Kate followed behind her silently. Mums stood in clusters, aperitifs and champagne glasses balanced.

Alexandra stared at the crowd of women, chattering about their families. Another life she could have lived.

"Have you noticed I can't do small talk?" Kate whispered to her as they sat on the seats fanning out from the dining table.

Alexandra whispered back. "You were kinda Bolshie with that poor woman! Suzan's harmless."

"In an 'I'm so busy and successful way'. If she had any more plums in her mouth, she could cultivate her own orchard. I can't stand that female role play." Kate motioned to the table. "Look at the altar to consumerism they've set up. Maybe they'll slaughter the mum who spends the least, as a ritualistic gesture. I intend to buy the smallest thing possible, so it could be me."

Alexandra whispered. "Can't you just take it at face value? Does it always have to be so confrontational with you?"

"It's my nature. I can't accept things blindly. That's why Katrina and I clashed over the years. To her this is a pleasant social gathering. To me, it's a cattle call to mindless living." Kate stared at the hostess, a jolly, rotund woman, who raised her hands for attention. "If you would all take your seats, I'll commence." She waited as they seated themselves.

"Good evening all," she continued. "I'm Ruth. Welcome to my talk on this great product. Firstly, I thank Katrina for the generous offer of her home this evening".

Alexandra glanced across at Katrina. She stood in the doorway, hunched over as Suzan spoke in her ear. They glanced at Kate and Alexandra looked away.

Kate fidgeted as she listened to the talk. After five minutes, she leaned across to Alexandra and whispered. "I'm dying here, I need a drink." She stood and headed to the bar. The Tupperware hostess hesitated as Kate's eyes appraised her.

Alexandra sat, mesmerized by the look in Kate's eyes. Kate replenished her glass frequently, all the while holding the gaze of Ruth.

Ruth handed out pamphlets to the group.

Katrina walked across to Kate. "Here's one for you. Don't think you can escape because you're at the bar."

Kate took the pamphlet. "The Buddhist in me shrinks from opening it."

Suzan circled around her. "My husband flirted with Buddhism after his heart attack. It's the favoured choice of middle-aged men facing the void. Personally, I never understood the need for fashionable religions."

"It's not a religion, per se." Kate replied. "It's a value system based on humanist principles. And maybe you're not close enough to the void yet." She drained her glass. "But I think a couple more nights like this could drive you to it. It would me."

"What will you buy tonight?" Suzan continued on. "I have my eye on the meat marinating container. Sad but true, you really value your Tupperware as you get older."

Kate didn't reply as she poured another measure of gin into her glass.

"A depressive's drink," Suzan remarked. "They say you can tell character by what a woman drinks. I love champagne, it's such a light hearted drink."

"Good for you," Kate replied. "I like gin, it's the preferred choice of women who don't aspire to the social wasteland of Tupperware parties and comparative conversations. No," she leaned close. "I like my drinks bitter and my conversation inspirational. I've got fifty per cent of the deal at the moment, so if you excuse me, I'll wander back to my seat."

Alexandra watched as Kate approached. "Is everything OK?"

Kate spoke in a low voice. "Help me. I have to get out of here. I need to..." she stopped and clutched her arm. "Help me."

Alexandra nodded. "Meet me in the hallway. I'll say goodnight to everyone." She squeezed her arm. "Don't worry."

1973: The Child Partisan

"She's crying again." Pina tiptoed back to their bedroom. "At least they're not fighting." She sat at the edge of the bed and looked at Alexandra. "I think we should open our presents."

Alexandra sat cross-legged on the bed. "We can't. We should wait for Mama to get up. Let's go see her."

"No! You know she hates it when we see her cry. She'll be angry all day. Then Dad will start shouting at her that she's always miserable and it never finishes." Pina tugged at the blanket. "I hate Christmas. They only stop fighting because their friends arrive for lunch and then they start again when everyone leaves. I don't see the point of pretending in front of everyone." She tapped Alexandra with her foot. "You can have my presents, I'm gonna sit in here all day."

"OK, if that's what you want." She swung off the mattress and Pina lunged at her. "I was joking. Don't you dare open my stuff."

They tumbled on the bed, laughing as they kicked the sheets and pillows to the floor. Their bedroom door opened and Emilio peered inside. "Girls, sshh! Your mama doesn't feel well. Her nerves are bad this morning."

"Pop, it's Christmas Day! We're just mucking around."

"Be quiet! It's a holy day, not just for silly presents and games. Now, get changed. You can come to Church with me."

"I'm not going." Pina tilted her head. "It's a waste of time."

"When you are grown and out of my house, you can do what you like. But now, you are under my rule. No more talk. We leave in fifteen minutes." He held a finger to his lips and closed the door.

"Bloody Hell!" Pina threw a pillow at the wall. "I can't even breathe without him telling me what to do. I hate him. Bet he wouldn't speak like that if I was a son."

"Pin, we'd better get changed. By the time we come home, Ma should be OK and we can open our presents. Maybe she won't stay sad if we leave her alone now."

"I'm sick of tiptoeing around the house all the time for her, whispering because of her nerves. They don't stop shouting because of us. I bet none of my friends have to do this." Pina stood at the bedroom window and stared out at the sunny day. "I hate them."

"C'mon, get changed. It just makes it worse if you don't."

Alexandra pulled her favourite dress over her head and buttoned the press-studs. She smoothed her hair into place and scrounged for her sandals under the bed. Pina stood at the window, silently.

Alexandra opened the cupboard, pulled out a blue dress and held it out to Pina. "That blonde boy at church always stares at you when you wear this. You said you want an Aussie boy. Well, this will draw him like a magnet."

"You're an idiot." Pina took it from her. "I should brush my hair, too." She walked down the hallway, tiptoeing past Claudia's bedroom.

Alexandra stepped behind her. The aroma of percolated coffee permeated the hall. "Dad's in the kitchen," she thought. "I'll just peek inside their bedroom." She moved across the carpeted hallway and quietly opened the door. It moved a couple of millimetres and she leaned forward. The blinds were tightly drawn and the curtain pulled across. A sliver of sunlight lay across the bedroom floor, created by a shaft of breeze through the partially open window.

"Mama," she whispered. "It's me, Alexandra."

"Islata moi." Her mother's shape was outlined under the bed covers. "Buon Natale."

"Merry Christmas, Mama." She ran to the bed and hugged Claudia, who sat propped against her pillow. "Are you sad again? Did you have a bad dream?"

"No, darly. I miss my sisters at Christmas time." She stroked Alexandra's dress as she spoke. "It still feels strange to see summer clothes in December. Sometimes I shiver in the heat, I remember the snow of home."

"Don't cry anymore. You'll just feel sadder. Thing of something happy and maybe you'll feel better again."

"Islata moi."

"What does that mean?"

"Gold of mine."

"That's Roland nickname, too."

"Si, his mama called him that. It was at Christmas that he joined the Partisans."

"Wasn't he just a kid, like you?"

"He lied about his age. He was just sixteen, not eighteen. He joined in September. Alexandra, shh! Listen. Do you hear it?"

Alexandra was silent. The blind made a flapping sound against the window ledge. "What?"

"The cuckoo is calling in the back garden. It lives in the pine tree along the fence. Listen."

Claudia's face was dreamy as she lay back against the pillows. "Bird of my country, it calls to welcome the sun. My cousin could imitate every bird he heard, even the cuckoo."

"Did Roland go away during the war?"

"No, he stayed in the village. The partisans lived in caves up in the mountains, to hide from the Germans. We would bring them food and hide it in our clothes when we went walking. He would call out the cuckoo's song when we came near."

"He must've been pretty brave."

"He ran messages everywhere. To the next village, to the other partisans, everywhere they send him. He said he was never scared, it was too much adventure to be scared. I would shake when he tell me what he do. But he laugh and say 'Dila, I live under a lucky cloud, they always cover me when I need them'. I believed him." She continued. "He came to see us when he got his uniform. It was a hot day and the uniform was made for the snow time. He was all red in the face and my sisters laughed at him. He was angry and told them he wouldn't protect them if the soldiers tried to hurt them. Olivia told him that tomatoes didn't belong in the army." She laughed. "She could be a terrible girl. She was so pretty but she could make boys cry with her words. Roland said she was the devil in a dress."

"Did she get married?"
"Before I left Italy. She was like a Hollywood actress, so slim. But she had too many babies and now she is fat like a pig."
"Maybe Roland teases her now."
Claudia didn't reply and Alexandra leaned close to her. "Did he love you?"
Claudia looked away under her daughter's gaze. "I was just a girl of fourteen, too young to promise anything."
"Did you love him, too?"
Claudia was silent and Alexandra stared at her. "Well, you mustn't have really liked him much because you married Dad."
"We ran out of time."
"Are you ready, Alexandra?"
They both started at Emilio's words. He stood by the side of the bed, looking down at Claudia.
"The oven is on."
Claudia turned away on her side.
Alexandra watched as Emilio left the room. She bent low to Claudia's ear. "But you loved Dad, right?"
Claudia was silent.

Alexandra stood. The room seemed to spin around her and she leaned against the cupboard.
Claudia motioned with her hand. "Go with your father, I'm feeling better now."
"Don't tell me any more of your stories, I'm sick of them." Alexandra shouted. "I don't care about your sisters or your cousin. If they loved you, they would come to see you here. Maybe they got sick of you crying all the time."

Alexandra thought she could discern tears on her mother's cheeks. She ran outside and bent her head against the fierce sunlight.

Pina sat in the Holden parked in the driveway. Alexandra slid across to her.

Emilio took off with a jerk of gears before she had time to close the door. Alexandra stared at the house as they drove away. The blinds in her parents' room parted slightly.

The cuckoo was silent now. The row of pine trees against the back fence was bereft of birdsong.

Chapter 30

"When, Mum?"

"I don't know."

Rosemary sipped her sherry. "I'd like to know when you're going back to England as well. Have you had enough dinner, Isabella? Good, then I'll clear the table and bring in dessert. Don't get up, Kate. I can still manage on my own."

Kate looked at Isabella. "I know you've had a bad day at school, but you said yourself that it's getting easier."

"No! You don't listen. I just want to know when we're going back home. Dad says my school's rung to check. I don't want to lose my place."

"I don't want to go back."

"What?"

"I'd like us to stay here. It could be home for us."

"Without Dad?" Isabella stared at her. "Did you know this before we left London?"

Kate was silent.

"Answer my question."

"Yes." Kate looked away from the expression in Isabella's eyes.

"I won't stay. I'm going home!"

Kate grasped her hand. "Just hear me through."

"You cow, I'm calling Dad." Isabella rose from the table, knocking her chair backwards. She bent to retrieve it. Her tears blinded her and she stumbled over the chair leg and fell.

"Leave it, Dear." Rosemary stood alongside her. "Your mother can pick it up. It's the least she can do."

"Ignore her. Please stay."

"I won't. I hate you." Isabella ran out of the dining room.

"Leave her to me. I'll talk to her." Rosemary picked up the chair on her way out and Kate watched as she headed down the hallway. She heard muffled voices, then the sound of the bedroom door closing. She eyed the sherry. "I hate that stuff."

She walked across to the sideboard and searched the bottom shelf for a decent bottle. Kate lifted a bottle of brandy from the recesses and blew the dust off. She headed to the sitting room.

She saw the outline of her face in the mirror over the fireplace. Kate switched on the lamp and stood directly in front of the mirror. A lined forehead and lank locks reflected back at her. "How did I become so old," she wondered, "and so lost that I could ever need her again?" She poured a full measure into her glass and sat down.

She stared at the hunting prints on the wall. Each had dust encasing the frames. Strips of paint hung from ceiling cornices, resembling streamers from a long ago party. The clock chimed the half hour and a snapshot of her childhood blazed into her mind. She remembered lying on the rug as she lined her toy soldiers to attack an imaginary battalion hiding in the fireplace, in the depths of the charred logs. Her father's smiling face as he led the charge with her, his long legs tangled over hers as they commenced battle. The half-hour chimed their signal to attack.

Rosemary entered the room quietly, her glass of sherry re-filled. Her cardigan slumped over her shoulders as she sat in an armchair. "She'll sleep here tonight."

"She won't. We're heading to town tomorrow."

"Not according to Isabella."

Kate was silent as she refilled her glass.

"She feels betrayed by you, Kate."

"Well, isn't that fucking ironic coming from you!"

"Are you going to bleat on again about how I failed you as a mother? Can't you admit how hard it is to be a parent? You haven't treated Isabella with any decency yourself, the poor child's distraught. I would never have pulled you away from your father."

Kate leaned forward, knocking the brandy bottle over the coffee table. The liquid dripped over the table and stained the thick carpet below.

"Leave it, Mum! I'll clean it. At least it kills the museum smell of this room."

Rosemary stood.

"For fuck's sake, leave it!"

"You're as nasty as your father when you drink. His tongue was just as sharp."

"I'm nowhere near drunk. Not yet." Kate waved her to a chair. "Sit and talk to me. Why did Dad drink? Didn't you give him enough?"

"I don't have to listen to this nonsense."

"When did you ever act with any decency towards me? On the day of the funeral, you packed all his things away. I couldn't believe it."

"I had to do something. You kept creeping into the cupboard and crying into his dressing gown. I couldn't stand it any longer, my nerves were strained beyond belief."

"I needed something you wouldn't give me."

"I tried."

"You fucking didn't! I begged you for the Meccano sets but you hid them away. I just wanted to smell him again, to feel him in some small way." She lifted her skirt and pointed to a scar below her right knee. "Do you remember when you heard me screaming in the garage the Christmas after he died? You found me lying on the floor, covered in blood. I told you I cut myself on a tool I tripped over, but I didn't. I fell off the ladder trying to reach up to the shelves, looking for my Meccano. I knew you didn't want me to see them again."

"I told you where they were before you left for London."

"It was too late by then. I needed them long ago."

"Well, I thought it was best to put them away. I bought you a watercolour paint set that first Christmas. You loved to draw as a child, I thought it would give you pleasure. But you threw them back at me, crying petulantly for the Meccano. You didn't have the temperament to keep those old things, you needed to shake off the memories and start again. Like I did. I got a job and we kept the house, life returned to normal again." Rosemary's continued. "You wouldn't even do art for the H.S.C. It was like you wanted to ruin your life from the onset." She sipped her drink. "I'm not so bad now, am I? You've hurt your own child as much as you say I hurt you. A Meccano set isn't equal to what you've done."

Kate stared at the art deco mirror hanging above the fireplace. As a child, she thought it resembled the tail feathers of a peacock. Sections of cut glass fanned out in an elegant patina of mirrors. It had hung in that spot since she was a child. The wire string had rusted over the years. She motioned to it. "That's all you have from your mother, isn't it?"
"Yes".
Kate raised her glass and threw it. The mirror shattered, shards fell into the fireplace below.
Rosemary's hands gripped the armchair.
Kate stood. "I'll collect Isabella after lunch. Tell her I'll phone Nicholas and we'll discuss our future. I owe her that." She motioned to the mirror as she moved to the doorway.
"I hope that broke your heart."

Chapter 31

"The Empress is ill." Pina spoke in a low voice. "Don't talk about it in front of her."

Alexandra glanced at her. "Ma?"

"She had some blood tests this week. Pop said she's always tired, complaining of lower back pain. He took her to the doctor's on Monday and she checked her blood."

"It's probably nothing. She's always been a hypochondriac."

"About us, yes. But never about herself." Pina continued. "Ted thinks she looks ill."

"I haven't noticed."

"You're always around, he's not."

The back door opened and Claudia walked out to the back patio, carrying a tray of coffee and biscuits. "My girls."

Pina replied. "I love being called a girl at fifty two. What'll you call me at sixty?"

"A miracle."

Alexandra lifted the tray from her. "Sit. I'll serve." She stared as Claudia gripped the easy chair and eased herself down. Her hands rested on her lap, twitching.

Pina accepted her coffee. "So, does Frank fancy you?"

Alexandra replied. "He fancies anyone in a skirt."

"Bantering aside."

Claudia listened, her eyes moving from one daughter to the other.

"It would be really awkward at work."

"Read my lips. Does Frank fancy you?"

"I think so." Alexandra looked away. "But it's not gonna go anywhere."

"Why?"

"I don't fancy him."

"Poor guy. You've told me he's no oil painting."

"You've never met him and you're taking sides. He's a good bloke but there's no spark."

"Mmm."

"Don't do that to me. I've waited years to meet the right guy. I might as well have married one of the oily wogs Ma tried to match-make me with years ago. We'd have a tribe of children and I'd be miserable; but I'd be valid in everyone's eyes."

"Methinks the girl doth protest too much."

Alexandra kicked her.

"Ouch, you haven't done that in years!"

"And what about your kids? Over-indulged and under-achieving. A shining testament to your obsessive parenting."

Pina looked at the tiled floor but stayed silent.

"Don't smirk, Pin, you always do that. Did I ever tell you what I really think of Ted?"

Pina laughed aloud.

Claudia shifted in her seat. "We should drink our coffee now." She glanced at Pina. "No more words."

"I've barely said anything! She can insult me as much as she likes and you never say a word. I ask one simple question and you both bite my head off. It's been like this ever since I was a kid. Don't speak like that to Alexandra, don't do that to Alexandra, don't trigger the...." she stopped.

"You are tough, like your father. You do what you want, doesn't matter about anyone else." Claudia spoke in a low voice. "My Alexandra, she's different. Her heart is different, like mine."

"Thanks! I've walked on pins and needles my whole life around you both! I know you think she's more special than me, I knew that from my childhood." Pina bit hard on her lip. "But I've tried. I kept silent when I wanted to speak, watched you both whispering secrets to each other and pretended I didn't know. Why do you think I married so young? I had to get away, I couldn't stand it any more." She wiped her eyes and stood.

Claudia spoke softly. "My daughters, I tell you both everything."

"Not everything. What about the blood tests?"

"Pah! Emilio, he worries for nothing. My arthritis, that's all."

"Pin, sorry! We never meant it to appear like that," Alexandra grasped her hand. "You weren't as patient as I was when Ma was depressed. I thought you knew that's why she talked to me. You were so restless as a kid. That's it, isn't it, Ma?"

Claudia nodded.

Alexandra held Pina's hand tightly in hers. "I wrote to him."

"When?"

"Last week. I included my email, fax and phone number. If he doesn't contact me, it's not for lack of information."

"So what will you do if he doesn't contact you? Wait another ten years, I suppose."

"No. Franks thinks I should find out if he's a jerk. He's not, I already know that."

"Yeah. His past behaviour indicates that."

"Please, this is hard enough for me! I don't want you to think I shut you out too."

"I'm glad you did it. Life's too short for just one fling." Pina stopped and glanced at Claudia. "I think this is a good time for me to do the wash up." She winked at Alexandra as she collected the coffee cups. "Oops." She murmured as she headed to the back door.

Claudia's head was downcast in the morning light. Brown eyebrows were drawn onto her face by kohl pencil. The thick shape was startling against her lined face. In silhouette, the skin beneath her eyes appeared grey and drawn.

"What fling?" The words barely audible.

"It was nothing," Alexandra hesitated. "I meet a man in London, on my last trip."

Claudia stared at her.

"Ma, I'm forty nine years old."

"You never told me."

"He was a friend of Kate's. We knew each other for six weeks. It was no big deal, really."

"So, it was just before...."

"Yes."

Claudia spoke softly. "When I left Italy, I left my sisters behind. I waited for you and Pina to grow up, so I can tell you everything in my heart. But you don't tell me...."

"It's not like that. You moved to Australia to start a new life, a big life where you left everyone you loved behind. But it made you afraid for us, every step we took, we took with a caution. Be careful, think, you could hurt yourself. Stop, stop, stop!" Alexandra paused. "I needed to do things and not tell you, so you wouldn't be afraid."

"I see." Claudia looked straight ahead as she spoke. "Did he love you?"

"Yes."

"And you?"

"I loved him too."

"And..."

"And nothing. We didn't stay in touch and it was soon over."

The sound of clippers in the back garden, as Emilio trimmed the hedges. Small branches fell in clumps, their leaves vivid green against the drought-withered lawn.

"You must hate him now."

"Why? He didn't do anything wrong."

"He left you."

Alexandra remained silent.

"The Cuckoos have gone." Claudia stared at the row of pine trees that lined the back fence. "Every Spring and Summer they nest here. But I don't hear them this year, they must have moved away. I miss their song."

"Maybe they're a bit late this year."

"No, they always welcome the Spring." She stretched her legs and Alexandra saw her wince as she spoke. "They are a bird I don't understand. They leave their eggs in a strange nest for other birds to raise. How a mama can do that, I don't see is possible." She stared at the ring of trees as she murmured. "Bird of my country, always comes to welcome the sun."

Chapter 32

"Bah, humbug."

Chris leaned on the table. "Don't be a wet sock, Frank. Open your present. With love from us to you, the only Bank Manager who hasn't achieved his sales targets in five years."

"That's because you bloody lot won't cross sell." He looked across the restaurant table at his staff. "I'll be retrenched and living on the streets this time next year."

Alexandra replied. "Bah, humbug, Frank. Now open the damn birthday present."

He pulled at the wrapping paper and stared at the leather bound book in his hands. He sneezed.

"It smells."

"It doesn't," Alexandra protested. "It gets a certain aroma as it ages." She lifted the book from him and held it gently. "It's an early 20th Century edition of Banjo Paterson's verse."

Chris spoke. "I told you to get him a carton of beer."

"I've been on the wagon the last two months."

"You won't get invited to any parties if people find that out."

"That's the idea. My brother-in-law's Boxing Day party, to be precise. I start thinking up excuses mid year."

"Bloody Christmas! An annual excuse to continue the fight you had with the rello's last year. The kids get sick of Mark and I fighting all the way home over who goaded who first." Chris winked. "Tell him that you're going away with Alexandra."

"I wish."

A murmur went through the table and Alexandra changed the subject. "Do you really hate the book?"

"Yes."

"It can be the one and only book in your bookcase. Impress the steady stream of girlfriends rotating through your front door. Better than FX magazine."

"You make me sound like a Lothario."

"Be flattered." Alexandra saw Chris nudge one of the girls.

Frank leaned across to her. "Here's our present to you."

Chris nudged him. "It's cute how your birthdays are in the same week. Cutely expensive."

Alexandra opened the small, beautifully wrapped package. "Chanel No. 5! Guys, you shouldn't have but I'm glad you did. I've worn it since I was twenty."

Chris lifted an eyebrow. "That's loyalty. Mark calls me a perfume whore, I'll wear any brand as long as it's new."

"I'm loyal to the point of boring. Pina's always said that."

"We love that about you." Chris gathered her handbag. "Guys, I've gotta run. Mark can't control the kids beyond a couple of hours, he thinks a block of chocolate and a stack of DVD's is good parenting."

Frank called for the bill and they divvied the amount between them. The group headed towards Pitt Street and Frank pulled Alexandra aside.

"Come for a drink with me, it's too early to go home on a Saturday night."

"You're on the wagon. Anyway, haven't you got a date?"

"I'm resting at the moment. I'm woman'd out."

"What am I? A turnip?"

"Just Alexy."

She elbowed him as they reached George Street.

"Night all, that was fun. We should celebrate my birthday on a monthly basis."

Chris called out as she walked away. "You just want to stockpile Chanel."

Alexandra waved as the girls walked towards the bus stop, giggling between themselves.

"Pounds to peanuts they're gossiping about us." She looked up at Frank.

"Hope so."

She looked away.

"Let's go for a walk." He pulled her closer. "Get some good city smog in our lungs."

"To Hyde Park, then. About face, you're going in the wrong direction."

"I've heard that before."

She replied. "Don't be pathetic."

They strolled past the Capitol Theatre and crossed over to David Jones. Alexandra stopped in front of an elegantly lit window. "My mama loves this store. She'd bring us here when we were little. We'd catch the red rattler to town and she would stand the whole way, so she wouldn't crease her dress. David Jones was the temple to high living in the sixties. She said it was the only shop that reminded her of Italian fashion."

"How's she doing?"

"Not so good. They're doing a battery of tests on her at the hospital, to see how far the cancer's spread." She stopped. "Frank, I'm gonna look for something in the Botanical Gardens." She strode ahead and crossed over to Hyde Park.

Lovers lay in grassy nooks. Lovers' time hung in the air, sweetly slow. Alexandra increased her pace. A wind picked up from the harbour, blew leaves into the pathways. A kookaburra sounded above her, its feathers shook as the guttural call sounded.

"Forget me not" she whispered.

Frank huffed behind her and she turned to him. "We might see a Shakespeare in the Park play, they do that in the summer."

"A couple of guys poncing about in doublets and tripping over possum poo. Doesn't do it for me."

They neared the Domain and her step slowed. Creamy trunks of ghost gums were lit by sunset hues and a swooping line of cockatoos screeched above. Their call echoed across the harbour.

Picnic rugs lay scattered across the grass at the Domain, as families chattered over tea lights and hampers. The expectant buzz of the crowd matched the deafening cicada calls.

"What're you looking for, Alexy?"

"A tree."

"In a park? I'm pretty sure you'll see at least one."

"Very funny. It's a particular one, a bottle tree near Farm Cove. Edward climbed it as a child."

"The English wanker? You're gonna sit in it and cry into your lace handkerchief for your lost love."

"I wouldn't be that stupid. I just want to see it."

"When it comes to men, women park their brains at home."

"Thank you."

"I'll chop the tree down with my bare hands if it'd knock some sense into you."

"That's damage to public property. You'd get arrested."

"I'll sever a couple of branches then, as a symbolic gesture."

"Much more intelligent. Where would you hide them?"

"Behind you, of course."

"Chivalry reversed. Now, try to look normal. We're entering the gates."

Alexandra paused at a fountain. Its pale stone was still hot to touch and she bent and swirled her hand in the water. The motion stained the inner stones a deep grey. Behind a mass of trees, the dark blue of the harbour glinted in mosaic-like fragments.

"You ever seen it before?"

Frank's words roused Alexandra from her reverie. "No."

"You couldn't have cared for him that much."

"Playing Professor Freud again?"

"Yes."

"Well, you'll be glad to know I'm trying to make it real again." She gave a brief laugh. "Or should I say, at last?"

"I see. Professor Freud feels you are on the precipice of change."

"What do you think will happen next, Professor?"

"You'll snap out of your delusional state and meet a tall, balding man who suits you better."

She bent her head. "Have you turned into a clairvoyant or did Freud dabble in tarot readings on the side?"

"It was the next logical stage in his career, I'm told."

They walked on silently. Cockatoos trailed through the grass, their pink feathers raised questioningly as they approached. Alexandra searched the tree line ahead.

"There it is, Frank!" She ran ahead and patted the quaint, bulbous truck of the bottle tree.

"He was here," she whispered. "My transplanted English boy."

Frank approached quietly behind her as she grasped a branch to climb up. "Let me help you." He doubled over and pointed to his back. "Use me, just take your shoes off. Stilettos always leave a terrible mark on my skin."

"This is good of you."

"I'm a bloody idiot but it takes one to know one."

"I wish I'd left my stilettos on now."

He grunted. "Hurry up, you're no featherweight."

"Takes one to know one."

She swung across to a branch and clambered onto its sturdy frame. "I hope this isn't illegal."

A jogger passed by, gazing at Alexandra, bemused.

She flushed as she studied the bark. Initials and words were scratched into the wood, weathered by wind and rain. She peered in the twilight for a name. "I can't find it."

"Find what?" Frank called out from beneath her. "Did he leave a toy behind?"

"Very funny. Edward carved his name into the tree."

"Bloody twit. Didn't he know that's illegal?"

She stared at the landscape. She imagined the white sails of Bennelong point arising from the mass of concrete and cranes, as the distraught little boy carved his name into his city's memory. "Forget me not." She whispered again.

A cockatoo took flight and the flock followed. Their screeching pierced the silence.

Alexandra jumped down and picked up her shoes. "C'mon, let's go for that drink."

She walked on barefoot. Then turned back questioningly. "What're you waiting for...." Then stopped. "Frank," she gasped, "you can't urinate in a public place."

He turned to face her. "Professor Freud says it's important to have closure. I'm just taking the piss out of the English for you."

She smiled as they walked back to the city.

Chapter 33

Alexandra placed the tray on the outdoor table. Kate squinted in the morning light and motioned to the pots. "New plants. You're expecting guests."

"The oldies are coming for lunch tomorrow. I've given up bush walking now Mum's undergoing the chemo. Pina and I are taking it in turns to cook Sunday lunch for them."

"I'd never do that for my mother. I know how much you love yours."

Alexandra was silent as she sat down. She poured their tea and offered the biscuit plate to Kate.

"Why not?" Kate took a jam tart. "Mother told me I've put weight on my hips. Said Nicholas wouldn't recognize me if he saw me."

Alexandra laughed. "You'll always be guaranteed to weigh less than me."

"Thanks." Kate squeezed her hand. "I'm sorry, must have been a huge shock for you. How long's the chemo for?"

"A couple of days. It's spread to her lymph glands, so...." Alexandra swallowed. "It's worse if I'm visiting Mum's place. She's always been such a dynamo. When I was a little girl, I thought she was superhuman. I thought she would live forever and always take care of me and Pina. Dad walks around like a little boy, who needs someone to hold his hand. " She continued on. "Sometimes, when I'm in the kitchen, I look outside and I catch her expression, unawares. She's lying on the cane rocking chair and she looks so frail. Like her mortality's slipping away and she's accepting it. I..." She paused. "I remember once, in Primary School, Pina snuck into my classroom. She'd spilt glue on her hat and didn't know what to do. Mum was in hospital for the week, resting because of her nerves. We both sobbed like babies. We knew the only person that could fix Pina's hat was gone and we were lost without her." Alexandra shrugged. "I know it's silly, but I get the same feeling now when I watch her."

"Is her spirit strong? What's she said about it?"

"Not a word."

"Cut of a different cloth to us. My mother would be exactly the same."

Alexandra went to speak but stopped.

"But I don't love my mother like you do. That's what you were going to say."

"You're still a prophet."

"I exist to make other people feel uncomfortable." Kate squeezed Alexandra's hand again. "I needed to be here today."

"It's not often that someone needs me!"

Kate shook her head. "God didn't give you those eyes for nothing."

"Kate, I've never heard you mention God before! Are you going through a religious crisis?"

"Do you know who I saw the other day? The Christian boy I lusted after at Uni. Bumped into him at Ultimo on the bus."

"Is he still gorgeous?"

"In a married kind of way, yes." Kate leaned back in her chair. "Imagine, living your whole life in the shadow of the cross."

"You asked him?"

"I could tell. He had the same otherworldly face of twenty-five years ago. And he has five kids and one wife."

"One exhausted wife."

"Yes, but what a sex life!"

Alexandra took a sip of tea. "Where's Bella today?"

"With Mother." Kate hesitated. "She's stayed with her since the night I told her I didn't want to go back. Did I tell you that Nicholas is coming to Sydney?"

"No!" Alexandra sat upright. "Is that a good thing?"

"I think it's a final thing." Kate looked down. "I called him on Monday. Isabella's homesick and at her wits end. I haven't told her the truth about coming to Australia."

"What's that?"

"I don't know myself," Kate spoke softly. "When I disembarked from the plane, the light lured me. It was like gauze had been removed from my eyes and I could see again. That doesn't make any sense, does it?"

"You're bloody lucky Katrina didn't hear you say that. Are you invited to her cocktail party?"

"After the Tupperware fiasco? You are, of course."

"Of course, observers are always welcome at social functions. We re-enforce everyone's normality."

"We all play roles. You're the observer, I'm the difficult one."

"Maybe we all fall into roles because it's too difficult to be who we really are."

"Now that's a sentiment worthy of me, Alexandra. Be careful what you say in front of Katrina, she'll think I'm warping you."

Alexandra lifted her eyebrows.

"But there I go again, labelling you." Kate stared at the lawn as she spoke softly. "I can't live with role playing again."

"What will you say to Nicholas?"

"I don't know. He's angry with me, as are Isabella and Mother. Maybe I'll run away."

"I thought that's what you did when you came here."

"Lifelong patterns are hard to break." Kate sipped her tea. "I'm tired of feeling lost. The only place I ever felt at home in London was the National Gallery. It thrilled and intimidated me at the same time. It was like being in the home of a forbidding great aunt. You loved the knick-knacks you found in her home, but her presence left you immoveable. Does that make sense?"

"No, but I'm used to that from you."

Kate rubbed her hand on the chipped vanish of the table as she spoke. "Do you ever wonder what might have been?"

"All the time," she whispered.

Kate waved her hand at the flat. "It's delightful here, but did you ever wonder what it would have been like if you moved in with Edward?"

"He told you?"

"Yes."

Alexandra fell silent.

"You never speak of him."

Alexandra looked up. "Neither do you. When we met at the airport, why did you ask me if I'd received any letters from him recently? You must have known the answer."

"I don't know. Maybe I wanted to provoke a resolution for someone else. I'm not brave enough to solve my own problems."

Alexandra reached into her bra and pulled a tissue out. "That's where Ma always puts her tissues. Apple hasn't fallen far from the tree, has it?"

Kate spoke in a dreamy voice. "It's the same when you lose a parent when you're young. I remember just looking for something that Dad had touched. Anything, a tea cup, a plate, anything to bring back the scent and feel of him." She continued. "But Mother had erased him, I couldn't get a sense of him anywhere."

"I'm sure she did with the best intentions. She's a product of her times, a no nonsense British disposition."

"It was cruel," Kate whispered. "Like he didn't exist at all."

"So what do you remember of him?"

"The shed, we spent hours in there."

"I can't believe you had a dad that played with you. Mine always seemed to be in the garden. It was like he was running a small farm. Or he was hammering and building something for Ma."

"My dad wasn't good with maintenance. I remember Mother always complaining that something was broken and he wouldn't fix it. He just liked to potter in the shed with me." Kate waved her hands as she spoke. "We'd get up early on a Sunday morning and creep into the shed. It would be in complete darkness and Dad would switch the light on. The bulb made a buzzing sound as it spluttered to life. Then he'd pull a Meccano set down from the top of a shelf and I'd sit on a high stool beside him and we'd lay the pieces out in neat rows. I'd screw them together as he read from the diagram. When we'd finish a structure, he'd place the battery in and I'd sit on his lap and watch the model come to life. He'd caress me and call me his girl....." She stopped. "You see, I have loved a parent as much as you do." She lifted her saucer from the table. "This was lovely, Alexandra. I must have you over for a visit. The flat's a bomb-shelter though, my sketches are everywhere. Isabella says the only uncluttered place to sit is on the loo."

"Do you miss her?"
"No." Kate glanced at Alexandra's face. "You're probably shocked by that. All good mothers should miss their children. I sketch more now that's she gone. If she wants, she can go back to live with Nicholas."
"To England?"
"Yes." Kate shrugged. "You must think me heartless but I need this time. If I have to, I'll give her up." She turned away as she spoke. "I was raised with generational callousness."
Alexandra spoke softly. "I think I understand."
"Thank you." Kate stood. "I need to go." She lifted her handbag and kissed the top of Alexandra's head, then fled down the driveway.
Alexandra listened till the sound of her footsteps faded away.

Chapter 34

"Ma will eat her dinner later, Pop. She's not hungry now."
Emilio turned away from cleaning the barbeque and stared at Alexandra.
"She's OK, just tired. I'll eat with you now. We always do justice to a plate of fish." She smiled at him. "C'mon, we'll clean up later." She pulled him away and he followed her to the patio table. Alexandra stared at his hands as he sat across from her. Varicose veins knotted the surface like blue strands of rope.
"Those hands planted vines, made wine, crafted wood." she thought. "They look so old and feeble now."
She spoke aloud. "Ma looks better today. I don't think she'll have to go into hospital this week."
"This week, next week....." He muttered. He stared at the garden as he spoke. "She wants to die here."
"Oh, Pop!"
"She does, with you and Pina and me here."
"The Specialist said the cancer wasn't spreading as fast as he thought. We don't have to think about that for some time."

"You are a child of peace-time, you never had to think of the future. Your mama and I, we always think. What we do if we are sick, if we die young, who look after you and Pina? No family here to help us in a new country, no English words to say how we feel. We think too much, always worry thoughts, because we have no peace."
Alexandra squeezed his hand. "You have us. The past is gone."
"But not our memories. We work hard in this country and the worry destroy our peace. But in this house, Claudia has peace. No one can take it away from her. She can die here."

Alexandra bent her head, unable to hold the blazing look in his eyes.
Emilio drank his wine and refilled the glass. "I drink for courage."

"You don't need to. You're the bravest man I ever knew."

He spoke as if he didn't hear her. "They gave us away when we were children."

"Who did?"

"Our parents, they gave me and Claudia away."

"What are you talking about? Ma's never said anything about this."

"We never talk about it but we always remember. Our parents had nothing during the depression, no food to feed our brothers and sisters, so they send Claudia and me away. Every family did it, gave one or two of their children to their parents, to keep for a few years. But they don't know what we suffer, how much we miss them." Emilio stared as the wind blew the corn stalks, the silken ears mirroring the sun's gleam. "We lost our families long before we got on the boat for Australia."

Alexandra was silent as he spoke. "I lived on my Nonni's farm. Claudia lived in the same valley. We would meet near the spring and cry together. Claudia, her nerves never come good again. I tell her that one day, we run away together and not come back. We find somewhere safe, to be forever there and not pushed this way and that way....."

"What did she say?"

"I asked her to marry me when she was twelve. I said we have the same memories, the same heart, so we should be together always. She wasn't ready, she said she would think about it". He smiled. "She made me wait long time for my answer, till after the war. She tell me she is ready to leave her village. Ready to make a new life. I wait ten years for her."

"You must have loved her greatly."

"Her heart was my heart, I wait for her to see." He stared at Alexandra with unblinking eyes. "When I see her again, she shakes so bad. Her nerves gone. Like our old lives."

"Did you ever ask your parents why they chose you? Did Ma ask her family?"

"We ask no questions in that time, we obey and cry where they don't see us." He watched a crow land on the grass nearby, its black head tilted towards him. "Claudia has peace here." He lapsed into silence as he ate his meal.

Alexandra watched him. The sparse, white hairs on his head were matted together by sweat.

"You gave her a good life, Pop. You can be proud."

He looked up at her words, then nodded. "She was my everything."

In The Tunnel

Alexandra stood. "I'll check on Ma, see if she needs anything." She walked into the darkened house and tiptoed down the hall. The radio on the kitchen bench tuned to Italian news, as it had for the last thirty years.

Alexandra opened the bedroom door. The blinds were drawn and an eerie half-light lit the room. Betwixt dusk and dark.

Claudia's hands rested on the bed-cover and Alexandra stared as they trembled on the linen. Thin, white hands.

"Just like Dad's," she pondered, "they've cooked feasts, made dresses and curtains, caressed and soothed. Worn out now."

She moved to the side of the bed and perched on the edge.

"Darly." Claudia lay with her eyes open.

"Did you sleep?"

"A little." Claudia sat upright and leaned against cushions that Alexandra placed behind her.

"Alexandra, my pins."

Alexandra opened her dresser drawer and collected a handful. "Like old times" she thought as she placed them on her mother's lap.

Claudia pointed to herself. "Do I look ugly?"

"Never."

"You stare at me like I am a ghost. I have no strength to colour my hair."

"Pina and I can do it for you tomorrow. We'll have you looking like La Loren in no time."

Claudia stretched out an arm to touch Alexandra. "You and Pina, always with your jokes."

"Why don't you come out to the patio, it's warmer."

"No, I like it here." Claudia looked at the deepening shadows. "I always love this time of day in summer. The sun not burning strong, like during the day. I could walk in the garden, cut some roses and water the soil. I love the smell of night in Australia."

Alexandra gathered Claudia's hand in her own. "Pop told me what happened to you both during the Depression. Why didn't you ever tell us?"

In the shadows, Claudia's eyes were impenetrable. "A story of long ago. I cried so many tears, like Emilio. We had no heart left to tell the story."

"Must've been awful. Did your parents send you far away?"

"No, I lived not even a kilometre from them. Nonni's farm was on the first hill looking down at the village. I could see Mama's kitchen chimney from my bedroom window. When I saw blue smoke, I would run down to the village and hid underneath the windowsill. I could hear Mama laughing with my sisters as she cooked. I wondered how she could be without me. But I didn't make a sound because I knew Mama didn't want me back, not until Papa came back from the sea. I ran away once from Nonni and Mama screamed at me and sent me back. She said I was a child of sadness and she had enough, without mine too." Claudia shook her head. "It's not good to talk of such things again. But I always wondered....."

"What?"

Claudia kissed Alexandra's hands and was silent awhile. "I can tell you anything, my daughter." She looked away as she spoke again. "When she sent me away to live with Nonni, I never knew if it was because Mama loved me the least or the most of her children. I wondered that all my life." Her hands shook and Alexandra pressed them close to her heart.

"Remember when I was little? I would pester you for stories about your life in Italy. You never told me the rest of the story about the boy of gold."

Claudia stared at Alexandra as she spoke. "I didn't want to hear about him when I was an obnoxious teenager. Then I grew up and forgot about him." She kissed Claudia's hand. "Tell me what happened."

Claudia was silent awhile and Alexandra waited.

"Where's Emilio?"

"He's outside, cleaning the barbeque."

Claudia lay back amongst the pillows and pressed Alexandra's hand. "You still have an old heart, made for listening." She spoke on. "No-one remembers him now. His family are all dead." She closed her eyes and seemed to drift into sleep.

The twilight faded and darkness engulfed the bedroom.

"No, leave the lamp off." Claudia grasped Alexandra's hand with surprising strength as she turned to the bedside table. "It's better."

Her voice was firmer. "If I tell you, he will live in someone's heart again......"

Alexandra waited.

"My sisters and I would steal fruit from farms in the summer time."

"What! You were so strict with Pina and I if we did something wrong as kids."

"But you were never hungry as a child." Claudia continued. "Oliva was the worst of us. She would cut branches from fig trees and pull them to our hiding place. We were laughing so much at her. She would get angry and say we leave her to do the work of a criminal and we get the benefit."

Alexandra could tell her mother was smiling in the dark. "Roland was with the Partisans that summer. We took them fruit every Sunday, we hid it in the drains outside the village. They would leave us flowers to say thank you. Oliva would blush every time she found a flower and put it in her hair. Such a silly girl."

Claudia cleared her throat and Alexandra handed her a bottle of water.

"Thank you, Darly."

Alexandra waited.

"Roland left me the purple flowers I loved. They only grew high in the mountains, where the Partisanos were hiding. He made the lettter 'C' with rocks and put them in the middle, so I knew they were mine."

"He did love you, Ma."

Claudia was silent and Alexandra pressed her hand.

"One Sunday, we come late to the drains. Oliva is bitter angry with us, because we don't help her again. She scream at me that I am lazy and throw the branches at me. I pick them up and as I stand I see a long gun in front of me. How you say this, Darly?"

"A rifle."

"Si. And a German soldier stands in front of me with his gun. The soldiers watch us for weeks, to see why we come. And all they see are two tall, skinny boys, to come collect the fruit. The soldier scream at me to tell who the boys are. I am frozen to speak. He puts the gun into my stomach. And Roland, he scream for me to run inside the drain with my sisters. The Germans, they look to see where his voice come from but he don't care. He run towards me and pulls me to the drain, screams at my sisters to come. I don't want to let go of his hand but he make me. I feel him shaking as he touch me, and I beg him to stay. The Germans don't know who he is, I will say he is my brother. But he bend down and smile at me and the sun is shining on his golden head. He hold my hand and I feel it shaking again, with his life blood inside. Then he let go and I start to shake with my hands. He stands up and talks to the Germans and they are shouting at him. My sisters and I, we can't breathe, we are so frightened. Then, we hear guns and screaming and then all is silence. We stay inside the drain long after we hear the soldiers laughing as they walk away."

Claudia stopped and Alexandra held her hand tightly as she waited.

"My sisters climb out first but I already know he lives inside me." She stroked Alexandra's hand as she spoke and Alexandra bent to hear her words.

"The sky is so blue and the flowers so beautiful in the fields, that I think there must be a mistake. How can so much blood come from two boys? How can so much beautiful flowers exist in such ugly death? I run to him and shake him but he doesn't move. He is still, even his hair is stained with blood."

Alexandra wiped her eyes but didn't intrude on her mother's words.

"His mama didn't cry when they bury him. I watch her and I don't cry, too. We cry inside our hearts, where no one see. She hug me at the church and say I will always be her daughter, even without his ring." Claudia's voice faltered briefly. "She said a silver bullet went straight through his heart. Only a precious metal could take her boy of gold away."

They sat in the bedroom in silence. A mild wind blew the drawn blinds, creating a whistling sound.
"Close the window, Darly. Too much air will make the room cold."
Her hands lay on the doona cover. Even in the darkness, Alexandra could see them shake in their nervous prison of worry.

Kate held her charcoal pencil aloft, her lips pursed as she stood back from the easel. "The perspective's wrong," she thought. She pulled the canvas sheet from the easel and shredded it into fine slithers.

She re-positioned the photo to the top corner of the easel and stared at the blank page. "Don't go away now," she prayed. "I need this." She stared at the fine lines that criss-crossed her smooth hands. She lifted the pencil with a nervy hand and commenced again. The strokes remained fluid and she breathed out in relief. "Thank you."

Outside her window, traffic and lawn mowers blended in suburban symphony. A shaft of sunlight stained the floorboards and Kate stared at the effect. She remembered the short path from her parent's house to the fibro garage, the feel of grass underneath her feet as she ran towards the haven of her father's arms. Her mother's disapproving face staring out from the kitchen window as Kate closed the garage door behind her and walked in the half-dark towards the workshop bench.

His warm caress on her body as she huddled on her stool. Warmth of his hand on her back, her thighs and between.

She stopped and stared at the canvas, her hand in mid-air.

Perspective shifted again in the sunlight.

Chapter 35

Isabella looked up as Kate opened the front gate. "My gerberas have flowered!" She held up a posy of pink and cream blooms.

"Shouldn't you be doing the weeding, and Grandma the flower arranging?"

Rosemary shifted on her gardening mat and pulled her gloves off. "She's like you," she remarked, "Isabella does as she pleases! The unpalatable stuff is left to grandma." She looked at Isabella. "She's so sweet, I let her get away with it. Be a love and put on a cup of tea." Rosemary readjusted her gloves. "No sense in sunbaking on the steps. You'll only burn, Kate. You have my complexion."

She continued to dig with her rusted fork. Isabella wandered through the garden, cutting over-ripe blooms and green stalks. Kate stood and entered the front hallway. Psychedelic shadows projected on the walls as her eyes adjusted to the change of light. The musty smell of a long-closed house pervaded the hallway as she turned into the back kitchen. She connected the kettle's plug to the socket and stared out the window. Gradually, her eyes focused on the dilapidated back shed. Its walls were grey after years of bleaching sun and rainstorms. Her hand rose in mid-air to lift the garage keys from the plastic hook on the wall. She stood, immovable in the face of memories. She turned to open the back door and walk outside but found herself unable to.

The kettle whistled and she reached for the cups and saucers. The grey presence within her peripheral sight as she poured the tea. The keys within her reach as she lifted milk from the fridge onto the bench. She bustled about; her back turned to the window, and then headed to the front garden.

Kate set the tray on the outdoor table. "Tea's ready."

Isabella ran up the stairs, her slim legs taking them two at a time. "It's too hot to do anymore gardening, Grandma. I'm going to watch T.V."

"As you please, Poppet." Rosemary eased into the cane chair, flexing her hands as she sat.

"Don't overtax yourself because you have Bella here. She's perfectly capable of entertaining herself after school, Mother."

"I don't. She keeps me alive."

"I've been remembering the most ridiculous things."

"You brewed the tea bag for too long. I like my tea weaker." Rosemary stared at the garden as she spoke. "What do you mean, remembering things?"

"I don't know, strange things. At night, I'll awake from a nightmare, covered in sweat."

"I don't dream anymore. Haven't for a long time."

Kate tapped her nails on the cane chair as she spoke again. "You're lucky. I can't sleep through most nights now. I'm glad Bella's staying with you, I'm not very sharp at the moment."

"You're too young to be suffering that. It's your conscience talking to you. You need to go home to London and work it out with Nicholas. Isabella needs a father. All children do. You lost yours too young and look what it did to you. Don't deny her the chance to grow up with a father."

"You asked me what I was remembering." Kate turned towards Rosemary. "When I dream or when I sketch in the late afternoon, I remember foreplay."

Rosemary looked ashen as she stared at Kate.

"When shafts of sun on the floorboards inch towards my feet, I think of foreplay."

"Kate, please!"

"Listen! I remember a hand on my thighs, between my legs, in shafts of sunlight through grey windows. Behind me was darkness, but near the window was light and pleasure."

"I don't believe a word you're saying." Rosemary held onto to her chair as she attempted to stand. Kate held her arm and kept her imprisoned. "What am I saying, Mother? I don't know myself. But as I sketch, I see these memories. I feel them." Kate continued. "They walk beside me everywhere. I'm shopping at Woolworths and I pass through the automatic doors and a ray of light illuminates my path and the memories come. I sit in a café with a work friend and the sun reaches over the table and I see a hand rub my arms. It has dark hairs and freckles and a voice whispers to me to be quiet. And enjoy. It's our special time together, in a special place. Why do I remember this? I've never done so before. But here, in this light and at this time, I remember." She let go of Rosemary and drew her legs up and wrapped her arms around them. "I don't know why."

"You always spoilt things as a child." Rosemary spoke quietly. "Every dress I bought you would be stained and torn within a week. Even the Meccano sets you made with your father were damaged. Your father despaired of you. And now, you want to spoil his memory for me." She stood and turned towards Kate. "You were too much to handle. Your father always said so, too." She moved haltingly into the house and Kate let her go. The sunlight seemed to follow Rosemary inside.

Chapter 36

"Who are you, Kate?"

She was silent as Nicholas stared at the lounge walls, his back to her. He bent close to examine a large canvas and his hair fell across his forehead in a thick, grey sweep. Kate thought back to the night she met him. The same sweep of hair covered his forehead in endearing earnestness as he bent towards her. They had sat huddled together at a party, as a loudspeaker on the floor beside them blared. "Fated not to hear each other even then." She thought.

"Twenty five years I've lived with you and you never picked up a pencil. And now this."

"But you knew I liked to visit the National Gallery."

"For God's sake, yes. Most Londoners' visit it at some stage. But they don't fill their walls with sketches and litter their lounge with paints and an easel." Nicholas turned and stared at her. "That's what artists do." He continued on. "It's like you moved countries and became a different girl and I never got to meet the first girl."

She remained silent.

He stared at the portrait of Isabella. "It's just like her," he murmured. "Young and graceful."

"She's mostly lived with Rosemary since we arrived." Kate spoke. "They're both furious with me."

"I saw her this morning and we talked. You're not coming back, are you?"

"No."

"So what do we do now?" He turned and stared at her and Kate shifted in her chair.

"I don't know."

He walked to the window and stared out. The sun illuminated his features and Kate noticed the deep lines that fanned from his eyes, to his mouth. "That curve really ages him," she thought " it would make a great profile sketch."

Nicholas waved a hand about the room. "You're even messier here than you were in Kensington. The flat's immaculate since you left."
Kate laughed. "You weren't much better. Have you taken up with a cleaner?"
He frowned and Kate stared as the sad lines etched into his face again. "It's the southern light," she thought "it sharpens everything."
Nicholas broke into her thoughts. "No, I'm paying one. I must have it looking decent for prospective buyers."
"What, have you listed it for sale?"
"Kate, I'd pay you the courtesy of consulting with you on that."

She looked away as she spoke. "How do you think Rosemary looks?"
"Old. Ready to fall off her perch."
"You don't know her. That indomitable old bird will outlive me."
Nicholas sat on the edge of the sofa near her. "Bella could always stay with me in Kensington. We could sell the flat when she finishes her studies."
"I've thought of that."
He stared at her, his eyes glittering. "You would just let her go, so easily?"
"Yes."
"I've never understood you. All the other mums I knew in Kensington took their children to the circus or art class. You were always so passive, you never gave her opportunities."
"I couldn't be that mum. I didn't have the energy to focus on her like that."
"You didn't have any bloody energy for us! For Edward, yes."
"Do we have to go there again? We both made mistakes, remember? Let's talk about what's best for Bella."
His voice rose. "Letting her move thousands of kilometres away from you is best for her? She's a teenager, she needs you."
"We can call each other and I can visit."

"Kate, listen to yourself. If she crying because a boy's rejected her, do you think a phone call will calm her? She'll already feel rejected by you, living on the other side of the world."

"God, Nick, you make me sound awful. I left my country for you, remember? All I want is some time, I don't know how long."

"Cut that pseudo-American psychological crap! You have a daughter that needs you and you don't have time to luxuriate. I'm not saying that we get back together but you should come back to England. She needs you at this age, she always has but you're so self obsessed, you don't see it. Or don't want to see it."

"That's not true! Did you ever think that a mother who lets her child stand on her own two feet and make her own decisions is a gift in itself? I think a walk in Hyde Park on an autumn day, examining the pattern of veins on a fallen leaf is more profoundly loving than shoving your offspring to violin or ballet class. I'm tired of busy women who raise children to be equally busy. I'm tired of the pretense, Nicholas." She pulled at the frayed cloth of the sofa. "She could always stay with me."

"And is Sydney any different?"

"No, it's the same ethos here."

"Then why stay?"

"Because it feels like home. London never did."

"Kate, you can't just change your mind half-way through raising Bella and move continents without consulting me. I love her too."

"I know you do."

"Then surely you can sacrifice a couple more years to ensure Bella's stable. She needs us both."

"Why don't you move here?"

"For God's sake! Stop dreaming. We married in London, bought a flat together, worked in London. They were the ground rules of our marriage. Isabella is English, she misses her friends and school, misses her old life. I know, I've asked her. She can't fit into your decision just because you're homesick. You're the one who took off on holidays with our child and went awol. Grow up, Kate."

She remained silent.

He sat beside her. "Isabella tells me you're on a short lease." He leaned closer and she moved away.

"You can live in the flat with her and I'll move into a bedsit again. She needs both of us."

"No more ground rules." She said the words so softly, Nicholas bent his head to hear them. "No more ordering of my life. I needed that for a long time, or at least I thought I did." She turned to stare at him.

"That's it, then? I'm to live with Bella on my own or visit her in Australia. All because you've changed." He walked across to the window and stared at the bright landscape. "I'm an English man, Kate. I don't belong here. I don't want to migrate because you offer me nothing in return, not a shred of security."

He moved across to examine a charcoal portrait. It was of an elderly man sitting in a chair. His face was sketched in profile, and his shoulders slumped as he stared into the distance.

Kate glanced across. "That's a resident of the nursing home down the road. He had a great face, strong lifelines. I wanted to capture his reflective gaze."

Nicholas ran a hand over the canvas and Kate thought she saw him brush his eyes before he spoke. "I never knew you," he whispered. "I think I would have liked this girl."

Chapter 37

"You're abandoning us." Alexandra stood in the doorway of the office.

Frank looked up from his desk. "Don't make me feel like shit."

"You will at Area Office. Everyone's obsessed with targets. I leave the weekly meeting depressed with all the sales clichés they throw at me. They won't get your sense of humour and you'll be completely friendless. Don't smile, Frank. I'm serious. How will you survive that corporate crap?"

"I won't."

"Then why transfer?"

"I need to go."

Alexandra gripped the back of a chair as she spoke. "We'll miss you."

"I know but if I don't go, I'll fall back to the old patterns of my life. Everyone's out the door at Area by 5.30 on a Friday night, so I can't use work as an excuse to stay back."

"I admire your decision. Even though I know you'll be miserable."

"Thanks. I feel better about my choice already."

She sat down. "You know I'm always forthright with you."

"Mostly you are." He spoke softly. "Of course they'll offer my position to you."

"God no! I'm happy in lower middle management. I like to be just mildly important."

"You're more than mildly important to me."

She flushed.

"It's OK." He spoke again. "Anyway, you should take my job, you know it backwards. If you don't, they'll send out a real wanker and the girls won't cope with a genuine boss. The shock would kill them."

"Why do you have to change?" She looked at him. "We're a good team. You do realize that no-one smokes dope on Chatswood's main street? And Chinese businessmen don't wear dreadlocks and nose rings? It'll be so bland, you'll go stir."

"Too much ringing endorsement of my decision will send me stir." He leaned forward. "Sorry about your mum. Jenny told me she's in a hospice now."

Alexandra nodded.

"If you want time off, take it. We'll get relief staff in. You don't have to take half-days."

"I need to keep something of my life normal." She shifted in her chair as she spoke. "Ma looks wasted, she has maybe a few weeks left. Pina, Pop and I stand around her bed and try to talk naturally but the words sound surreal. A nurse injects her as we talk about the garden or a doctor checks her blood."

Frank squeezed her hand.

"She looks so small when she sleeps. Pina can't believe it's the same woman who chased us around the garden in a fit of temper when we were kids." She laughed. "Poor Frank, I'm really downloading on you."

"That's what I'm here for." He pushed the tissue box towards her. "You look gooey."

She reached for a tissue. "Don't go."

"If I go or stay, things won't change between us." He leaned back in his chair. "We'll end up alone, you and I." He stared at her. "We've missed our chance. I'm pushing against the tide and you won't let go of a ghost. He'll pull your heartstrings for life."

"Are you trying to cheer me up?"

"I don't know why I'm saying this. Maybe I'm brave because I'm leaving." He tapped his hands on the desk. "I'll be braver still. Alexy, I love you. I have for the past five years. You aren't my romantic ideal, I don't believe in that crap. You're funny, loyal, strong and you live your life with integrity. I couldn't ask for more. And because I don't look like bloody Lord Byron moldering in his

Kensington flat, I don't have a chance with you." He leaned forward, his bald palate shining under the electric light. "But we could have fun together. I love to travel. I'm amusing, blunt to the point of brutality, so you always know where you stand with me. No romantic shadows on my soul. You've got nothing to lose and a house and a four wheel drive to gain."

She smiled. "Is that the good provider clause kicking in?"

He searched her face. "Yes, but you don't want that, you want to hang on to the memory of a frightened man and I don't know why. If I'd met you in London, I'd have walked on bloody glass to see you again."

She was silent and he stopped.

"So......." she trailed off.

"So there you have it." He interrupted. "And you?"

"Frank, I didn't know....."

"Of course you did. The girls know, they tease me about you constantly."

"I guess I didn't pay attention."

"You didn't take me seriously. Poor Frank, the fat bank manager. Always alone."

"No, I didn't see you like that."

"Then how?"

Her hands gripped the chair. Too late. Imprinted in her mind, the faces of Nick and Edward. The boy and the man before.

She turned to see if the girls were busy behind the counter.

"Relax, Alexy. They're OK."

"I feel awful. I didn't take your bantering seriously. No one's fancied me in a long time. I'm nearly fifty, for God's sake!"

"I don't fancy you, I love you."

She licked her lips. "No."

"Can you elaborate on that word?"

"This is a bad time for me. Maybe we can have this conversation another time?"

"Will you ever," he whispered, "have this conversation with me again? Or with anyone?"

"That's unfair! You don't know me that well."

"When do I ever hear you talk about someone? You keep it all so tightly controlled, you must be exhausted shutting life out."

She stood. "Stop right there, Frank. You don't have the right to summarize me like that. You sound just like Kate, with knowledge you assume about me. You're just guessing at my life."

"I'm not far off, I bet. Did you ever think to ring the English guy, just to talk to the poor man and give him some encouragement?"

"Poor man! He never wrote to me in all these years."

"Maybe he was afraid of what it meant to you. Or didn't."

"You don't know what it meant to me, so don't pretend that you do."

"But you still haven't told me how you see me."

She turned to leave.

"Please, I'd like to know."

Alexandra leaned on the chair, her eyes averted as she spoke. "Apart from your arrogant assumptions about my life, you're my best friend."

"I see. Well, that's a good basis for a relationship. When you're ready to think about it, consider me as a potential partner."

"Knock, knock."

They both looked up sharply, to see Jenny leaning against the door frame. "I've often wondered what you two talked about in this office. I knew it wasn't home loans but I wasn't expecting this." Her eyes twinkled as she looked at Alexandra. "Head Office on line two for you. I think they want to offer you Frank's job." She gave an arc smile as she turned to leave. "Personally, I'd prefer it if you took Frank's offer."

Alexandra moved to the door. "I'll take it outside."

Chapter 38

Alexandra scanned the grounds of the Botanical Gardens from her seat in the restaurant. The withering heat bore down on the lily pond ahead. Mother ducks negotiated roots and outsize fronds, with their nervous ducklings in trail.

She peered over the railing of their outdoor table. It seemed two classes of birds existed within the restaurant grounds. In the take-away section below, squawking birds heckled tourists. Their impatient beaks tapped tables in search of food scraps. In the silver service restaurant above, the sound of cooing birds came from the foliage of trees that framed the outdoor area.

She turned back to the conversation at her table. "The Hall of Mirrors again," she thought "this time it's Kate lined up against Nicholas and Rosemary."

Rosemary sat opposite, with Nicholas and Isabella seated on either side of her. To Alexandra's right sat Kate, twirling her glass of wine.

Alexandra smiled at Nicholas. "Thanks for inviting me today. Makes me feel like family."

"It was the least I could do. You've looked after my girls."

Kate held her hand. "She always has."

Nicholas rolled up his shirtsleeves. "I don't know how you survive this humidity."

Alexandra spoke. "March's the worst month. Did you enjoy Sydney?"

"It's good to see my suntanned daughter again. She's become a surfer chick, I'm told."

Isabella nudged him. "Hardly."

Rosemary spoke. "She'll miss it when she's back in England."

Kate remained silent as she sipped her wine.

Nicholas leaned back in his chair. "I guess this is as good a time as any to talk about that."

Kate glanced at him. "We'll talk about it later."

"No, now." Isabella's words came out in a rush. "I have a say in my life."

"Look, I'll go," Alexandra half stood. "I should head to the hospice soon. Pina's been there all morning. It's been great seeing you, Nicholas. I'm sorry we didn't meet up before on your trip."

"No, stay." Kate pulled her down. "Please."

"I'll stay for coffee."

"Do I need to ask permission to stay?" Rosemary looked at Kate.

"No, you don't, Grandma."

Kate spoke. "Too many opinions will confuse the issue but there's not much I can do about that."

"Don't be pathetic." Nicholas replied. "Our discussions always become circular because you're so negative. Let's work this out now."

She looked down as he spoke on. "It's late March and Bella's missed a great deal of school term already. She'll need tutoring to catch up in England, the curriculum is vastly different."

"Bella's doing well here."

"She's told me she's completely lost in certain subjects. Her knowledge of Aboriginal culture is limited at best, I'm sure you would agree." He leaned forward and Alexandra watched as Kate backed away. "We can fly back this weekend, Bella's school has held her place. In a couple of months, she'll be back on track. No long-term damage done."

"I'd hardly call a holiday to Australia long-term damage."

"And letting her fly home without you would fall into the same category?"

Kate flushed.

"Why wouldn't you come back, Mum?"

"Perhaps not straight away."

"Then who would I live with?"

"Your dad, of course."

"When did you decide this? Why didn't you tell me?"

"Bella, I haven't decided anything. I'm enjoying being back home and I haven't set a date on my return to England, that's all."

"You make it sound so innocent," Nicholas looked at her. "Leave you child so you can further your artistic career."

"Is that it, Mum?" Tears streaked Isabella's face. "You won't ever come back?"

Kate reached across to squeeze her hand. "This has become melodramatic. You make me sound cold blooded, Nicholas, when in reality I have no long-term plans. It's not fair, I don't think as logically as you do. I'm more spontaneous and emotive."

"You don't think at all. I don't want Isabella to live in that haphazard fashion, she'd be imbuing a bohemian spirit that hasn't got you far in life. You'd never supervise her studies, just free spirit your way through life and Bella would take on your characteristics. I don't want that for her." Alexandra gripped Kate's hand under the table as he continued.

"You compartmentalize everything. The unpalatable is always boxed away on the highest shelf in your mind and thus you never achieve anything. You've never kept a consistent thought in your life. You've been a Stoic, a post-modern feminist and now, a Buddhist. What next, Khabbala? Isabella deserves more."

"Even as a child she did that." Rosemary interjected. "Never focused on anything, even her art, which she loved. Threw away all her talents. Now, it's Isabella's turn."

"That's unfair." Kate whispered. "You always diminish me. Both of you."

Rosemary replied. "You can't blame us for everything in your life. You made your choices and you need to carry them through. That's what we did in my generation, we didn't decide halfway through that we didn't want to win the war or be parents anymore. You must grow up, Kate. It's long overdue."

Alexandra spoke softly. "If she's really unhappy....."

"Kate's always unhappy." Nicholas interrupted. "We step gently over Kate's unhappiness, her needs. I'm over it." He drained his glass. "Bella's coming home with me. You can take as long as you like to find yourself and in the meantime I'll raise our daughter. Come visit us sometime." He stood. "Bella, let's start packing your things. Rosemary, I can drive you home."

"Thank you." Rosemary accepted his hand as she stood. "You see, Kate, all you need is backbone to make a decision."

Kate watched as Nicholas paid the bill at the bar and Isabella led Rosemary out of the restaurant.

"You didn't defend yourself." Alexandra spoke. "I expected you to argue back."

"No point," The lines around Kate's mouth deepened as she replied. "I'll never be the woman they want."

Nicholas approached the table and leaned over to Alexandra. "In case you're wallowing in pity for her, let me give you something to think about."

Kate clutched his hand but he shook her off.

"Please don't, Nicholas."

"Our marriage broke down several years ago. I suggested marriage counselling, weekends away, all to no avail. I loved my daughter and didn't want to be a part-time father." He looked steadily at Kate. "But you didn't need me anymore. You were too busy fucking Edward to notice Bella and I." He turned away and they sat in silence at the table. Alexandra stood and Kate watched as she walked away.

Chapter 39

Alexandra stared at Pina uncomprehendingly. "Are they sure?"
Pina nodded. "The fair-haired nurse, I forget her name, said Mum's breathing had changed." She squeezed her hand as she spoke on. "They've moved her to a private room." Pina's brushed her eyes with her sleeve. "Do you know what I couldn't stop thinking about? Years ago, when I was walking home from Primary School, I found a chick on the ground that had fallen out of its nest. Do you remember that?"
Alexandra nodded.
"I took it home to Mum and we tried to feed it and keep it warm on the window sill. But it didn't survive. Mum hugged me and said it was the nature of children to feel sadness at small things. She said that when I grew up, I would know other sadness that she couldn't kiss away." Pina turned away. "I can't get her words out of my mind now."
Alexandra held her hand as they walked down a corridor of the hospice. Innocuous reprints of walled gardens and sweeping landscapes hung on white walls. Alexandra stared at them as they walked past.

Pina pushed at a door at the end of the corridor. It opened to a room engulfed in shadows. The drawn curtains and dimmed lights made Alexandra's eyes wince. At the foot of the bed, she made out a shrunken shape, then realized with a start that she was staring at her father.
"Pop, has she woken?"
He hunched over the cast-iron bed, his eyes on Claudia. "They put her to sleep last night. She suffered when you went home. They gave her drugs and she sleep since midnight. I stay with her all night."
Alexandra stared at the figure in the bed. It had Claudia's features, the long hooked nose, dark brows and thin lips. Her hair lay tangled over the pillow. She lifted her mother's hand and kissed it.
"It's not right," she whispered to Pina, "that they extinguish her spirit like this."

"Ally, they had to. The nurse said she would fight for breath at the end and try to speak. She said it was kinder to let her slip away in peace."

Alexandra stared, dry-eyed. "I wish she could open her eyes. I'd like to see them once more."

A nurse entered the room. He adjusted the drip, then shook the contents of the plastic container attached to it. He smiled at them. "She's not in pain now."

They nodded at his words and continued to stare as he filled in the chart at the foot of the bed.

"Which one of you is Pina and Alexandra?" They started at the question. "Claudia speaks about you all the time. She said she wouldn't be strong enough to say goodbye. Seems like an extraordinary lady." He turned to go.

"Can she hear us?" Alexandra called out as he held open the door.

"I'm sure she can."

"I'm glad." She whispered.

Emilio stood. "I need to walk for a few minutes. I'll go up and down the corridor. Call me if...."

Pina took his arm. "I'll go with you."

Alexandra listened as the door closed. The room was silent, as the drip splashed into Claudia's veins. "This is your last day, Mama. I'm glad I'm here for it." She smoothed Claudia's hair into a neat bun at the top of the pillow and smiled. "La Loren would approve."

She sat at the side of the bed and watched the white sheet rise and fall with her mother's breath. In the background, she could make out the shape of a tree branch against the windowpane. The dark leaves pressed against the thick glass.

Alexandra stared at Claudia's chest. The sheet ceased to move. She stared at her mother's hands. They were still, her tremor extinguished. She lifted an arm and felt the still warm limb. Her fingers travelled to Claudia's hand. The gnarled fingers lay motionless and she pressed them to her face.

"Is he with you now?" She whispered. "Has your boy of gold come back?"

....

A wide expanse of lawn, dotted with headstones. Here and there, bright stripes of colour and paper windmills denoted a child's grave.

A Catholic priest prayed over the white coffin, sprinkling oils as he bent over the grave. All the flowers Claudia loved most were scattered about. Roses and dahlias blended with the smell of upturned soil. A light rain fell and spattered the coffin.

Alexandra stared at the scene, detached.

Pina stood close to the priest, her eyes streaming. Ted held her tightly as she stood surrounded by her children.

Emilio looked a shadow again, ready to crumple.

The lawn was flat and bereft of trees. "An odd resting place for a mountain girl" Alexandra mused.

The priest concluded his prayers and the mourners huddled together. Alexandra made a sign of the cross and moved through the dark-suited crowd.

"Alexy."

She glanced upwards. "Frank! It's so good of you to come."

"You knew I would." He looked at her. "You aren't exactly turning on the lavish grief I'd expect from an Italian daughter. What gives?"

"It feels surreal to me. Pina seems to have all the tabs on filial grief today." She half-laughed. "Even today, she's the perfect daughter."

"You unworthy child." He walked arm in arm with her, until they reached the road. The crunch of loose gravel underneath their feet. Directly ahead, a ring of trees stood near the road. Frank pulled at his tie.

"Did you come from work?"

He nodded.

"How's it going?"

"They're wankers, one and all."

"Told you so."

"No-one likes told-you-so people."

She nudged him. "It's good to see you today."

"Where's the English chick? I thought she'd be here today. Gone back to England?"

She shook her head.

Above them, bird song sounded. Alexandra smiled at she heard the familiar call. She turned back to the grave site. Emilio had collapsed into Ted's arms.

"It's the cuckoo, Mama." She whispered. "It's calling you home, Empress." Her tears fell gently, indistinguishable from the light rain. Frank held her tight and she rested in his arms.

Chapter 40

Kate couldn't read the expression in Rosemary's eyes.

"Come in." She moved back as Kate entered the hallway. "Sit in the parlour, I'll get Isabella's things."

Kate watched as she headed down the corridor. Rosemary's stoop seemed more pronounced and she appeared to have aged in the last week.

She sat on the musty sofa and stared out the window. The magnolia tree was flower-less and sunlight filtered past the bare branches and spread over the carpet at her feet. Kate stretched her legs as she glanced up at the wall. The Art Deco mirror had been removed. A dusty imprint remained, outlining the mirror's shape.

"She's just like you, in many ways." Rosemary entered the room. "A forgetful, dreamy child." She held out the clothes. "She rang me last night and asked if you could post them to her. Some of her favourites, apparently."

"That girl has more clothes than she needs." Kate folded them beside her. "Thanks."

"A glass of sherry?" Rosemary moved to the sideboard. "I'm having one."

"Why not?"

"The house is so still without her." Rosemary handed Kate a glass and she sat in the armchair opposite. "I remember the Saturday after you left for London. I was retiring from work soon and I wondered if all my days would be like that. It seemed so long and lonely with you gone. I knew you would never return to live in Australia. It occurred to me that I had to make a new life for myself, or I would be alone and forgotten by the world. Fortunately, I knew I could do it, I'd done it once before."

"You mean when Dad died?"

Rosemary nodded.

"I'm sorry for the things I said last time. They're just bad dreams I have at night and I let them spill over to my waking day...."

"No, you were right."

Kate froze.

"I caught him, once. I decided to walk to the shed and see what you two got up to, it all seemed so secretive. Hugh didn't hear me coming because it was raining and the sound blotted out my footsteps. I walked across the grass towards the window of the shed. I remember thinking how good the rain would be for the lawn, it was turning yellow in the summer heat. You were on a stool and had your back turned to me. He was ....touching you. I must have gasped because he looked up and I'll never forget the look on his face. I ran back to the house and I stared at the grass as I ran. It seemed I would never be able to walk on it again, the touch of it was poisoned by what I saw." She drained her glass.

"Of course it's in all the media nowadays, child abuse and the like. But then, there were no reports of such things and nowhere to turn to for advice. I froze inside, I couldn't speak or talk to anyone. My parents in England would have me back, of course, but they were elderly and you were a child and you just adored him." She stared at Kate. "So I stayed. I thought he would be too scared to do it again..." Rosemary gave a mirthless laugh. "It seemed that in one careless glance, I had lost everything. Do you know what hurt me the most? I could never call him by his name again. We were civil to each other but it was over for us."

Kate made no comment.

Rosemary continued, she twisted her glass in her hands as she spoke. "He never recovered from the shock. His sickness was a relief for both of us. I cared for him to the end but I was no more than a nurse. The day of the funeral, I emptied our room of his things. I needed to reclaim my independence. You were a child, I prayed that you wouldn't remember any of it. I was wrong, apparently." She lapsed into silence.

Kate watched the sunlight splash against a wall.
The clock on the mantlepiece chimed the half hour and the melodic sound filled the silence.
"It was all a lie then." Kate spoke softly. "My memories of him, of all he meant to me."
"We both needed the lie." Rosemary stood unsteadily to her feet. "Excuse me, Kate. I need a nap after lunch, I feel quite worn down most days. Really, I didn't expect to miss Isabella as much as I do. She's quite taken my spirit away with her." She tapped Kate's arm as she passed her. "Just close the door behind you. It's self-locking." Rosemary paused at the doorway and turned back. "It wasn't all a lie," she whispered. "You and I survived. That counts for something, doesn't it?"
Kate didn't reply. She listened as the sound of her mother's footsteps receded down the hallway.

Chapter 41

Kate looked up at the knock. She wiped the charcoal smudges from her hand before she opened her front door.

"Alexandra!"

"I came to thank you for the flowers. They were beautiful."

"You could have called me. I don't deserve more."

"I know."

Kate motioned for her to enter. "You don't have to sit on any of my furniture. You can tell me off standing up."

"Something's different about the flat. What is it?"

"Bella's stuff is gone. She left on Sunday with Nicholas."

"So you're bereft too."

"Mine's by choice." Kate motioned to the sofa. "I'll make a cup of tea." She walked across to the kitchenette and busied herself with mugs and tea bags. "Mother contributed to the flowers. She wanted to come to the funeral but she didn't feel strong enough to say another goodbye in the same week. She misses Bella terribly."

"Goodbyes are harder at that age. How is Rosemary?"

"Beyond disgusted with me."

"And how are you?"

"Do you care?"

"Mostly I don't. But I had to come here today, I don't know...." Alexandra fell silent.

She stood and examined the charcoal portraits. Kate had extended string across the room, to hang more portraits. Alexandra ducked her head as she wove about the room. "You've specialized in charcoal."

"It feels natural to me." Kate carried the mugs to the dining table. "I sold some portraits at the Glebe markets on Saturday. Bit of a dream come true, really." She continued. "I assumed you wanted peppermint tea, with honey. I'm too nervous to ask you any questions." She sat and held her mug against her chest. "I'd offer you biscuits or food but I don't have any since Bella left."

"You must be too upset."

"No, too busy."

"Who initiated it?"

Kate looked away. "Between Edward and I? I did."

"Why? He was all I had and you took him."

"Did you really want him?"

"Does it matter? You were a married woman, for God's sake and you knew I loved him. Why?"

Kate looked down. "I had to do something unforgivable. It was like a compulsion to destroy everything in my life."

"You always give such lyric words to bastardly acts."

"Unlike you? But you lie to yourself and to everyone else."

"But I don't drag others down with me in the process."

"Oh really? What about Nick from Uni? He used to stare at you with hungry eyes, just waiting to hear what you were really like. Did you ever think he might wonder about you for the rest of his life? Edward waited for you to call when you got back, to tell him you got home safe. You promised but you never did."

"He could have done the same."

"Really? You made so many subtle remarks about the finality of the affair. The man is not big on self-confidence as it is. A card would have made a huge difference to him. He opened up his world to you but you never returned the honesty."

"You've really turned this onto me. I didn't do anything wrong."

Kate's face blazed in anger. "You were passive in the face of love! That's a crime, Alexandra. A kindred spirit is rare and one you love, rarer still. You let him go."

"I never had him."

"You weren't brave enough to try."

Alexandra sat down on the arm of the sofa. "Do you love him? Does he love you?"

"No, on both counts. But we needed each other for a brief time. I needed a final parting from Nicholas and he had to let go of you. Otherwise, he would have gone mad."

Alexandra was silent.

Kate stood upright. "I have something for you." She disappeared down the hallway, ducking portraits and string.

Alexandra watched Kate return, a battered white envelope in her hand. "For you, from him."

Kate returned to her easel and kept her eyes adverted as she worked on the sketch. The scratch of her pencil the only sound in the room. Her nerves strained to hear any reaction from Alexandra. Finally the sound of the letter being folded back into the envelope. Alexandra held it tightly in her hand.

"I've had it since I left London. He asked me to give it to you when I was ready. Now seemed like a good time." Kate continued on. "I'd like to ask for your forgiveness. I know I've never forgiven anyone in my life and I don't deserve it. But I need yours more than anything else in the world. You're too precious for me to lose." She held her breath.

Alexandra stood. "I need Frank. Can I use your phone?"

"Of course, it's in my bedroom. First down the hall. You can vandalize the room if it makes you feel better."

Kate turned back to her portrait. She rubbed a charcoal line with her index finger, until it became a soft blur under her gentle pressure. She glanced out the window and noticed the sun had moved higher in the sky. A patch of sunlight lit the floorboards near her feet. Perception altered again.

She shaped the outline of her subject's face, all the time straining to hear Alexandra's voice.

Finally, she heard a laugh and her shoulders relaxed.

"I'd love to, Frank. See you tonight".

Kate caught the exultant words. She glanced again out the window and stared at the brilliant landscape. "I'm sorry, Edward," she whispered, "the light took her away."

She sketched on, suspended in the wait for Alexandra.

www.ingramcontent.com/pod-product-compliance
Lightning Source LLC
Chambersburg PA
CBHW060144130626
46556CB00006B/2492